Closer All the Time

A NOVEL

Other Great Fiction from Islandport Press

Abbott's Reach
by Ardeana Hamlin

The Contest
by James Hurley

Strangers on the Beach
by Josh Pahigian

Stealing History and *Breaking Ground*
by William D. Andrews

Contentment Cove
by Mirian Colwell

Mercy
by Sarah L. Thomson

Silas Crockett
by Mary Ellen Chase

Closer All the Time

A NOVEL

Jim Nichols

Islandport Press
PO Box 10
247 Portland Street
Yarmouth, Maine 04096
www.islandportpress.com
books@islandportpress.com

Portions of this book have been previously published or excerpted in the following magazines: *Night Train*, *Germ*, *december*, *Zoetrope ASE*, and *Enizagam*.

First Islandport Press edition published March 2015

ISBN: 978-1-939017-49-9
Library of Congress Card Number: 2014911175

Dean L. Lunt, Publisher
Book jacket design by Karen F. Hoots / Hoots Design
Book design by Michelle A. Lunt / Islandport Press
Edited by Genevieve Morgan
Cover photo from iStock.com

Once again, for Anne

*"I swore to God I would never turn into you;
I'm getting closer all the time."*

—Nine Inch Nails

Contents

Acknowledgments

My thanks to Dean Lunt and the Islandport Press team: Michelle Lunt, Melissa Kim, Holly Eddy, Jennifer Hazard, Shannon Butler, Karen Hoots, Teresa Lagrange, Isabelle Hattan, and the office boss, Penny; special thanks to my editor, Genevieve Morgan, whose very first suggestion led to a much better book, and whose continuing counsel has been invaluable throughout. Thanks also to Melissa Hayes for her line-editing prowess and generous encouragement. And to Monica Wood, Susan Henderson, Ellen Cooney, and John T. Nichols for their early looks and suggestions. And finally I must acknowledge all those who wound up inhabiting these pages: those fumbling, gallant underdogs, those uphill climbers, those hidden-away longers and seekers, who, if the tapping goes on long enough, will sometimes come to the door and tell you a story.

Closer All the Time

Johnny

Johnny Lunden had ridden his old surplus Scout halfway to Portland, filling out applications and angling for interviews. That was always harder than working itself, and by noon he was more than ready to call it a day. But when he got back to Baxter—tired, windburned, and thirsty—he saw a HELP WANTED sign in the picture window of the town's new restaurant, and after throttling back to think about it, he went ahead and pulled the Indian over to the curb. On the sidewalk he ran his hands through his hair and smoothed his mustache.

What the hell, he thought. One more won't kill you.

His reward for that impulse was a painful half hour in a cluttered little office at the back end of the building, listening to Alva Potter expound on modern business philosophy. Alva had it all figured out: You had to be sharp, and you had to compete. Business was like war—to put it in a context that Johnny might appreciate—and he could be thought of as the commander whom the troops must follow.

"You with me here?" Alva said, chin raised.

Johnny couldn't help clicking his heels together lightly and saying, "Sir, yes, sir!" at this point, but the commander was enjoying the sound of his own voice so much that he barely noticed. Johnny managed to restrain himself for the rest of the interview and ultimately walk away with an application in hand and Potter's man-to-man pledge—Johnny had to bite his tongue here—to give him fair consideration.

On the way out Johnny swung by the bar to reconnoiter the work space. He liked that it was going to have a sports theme, with an emphasis on fighting, boxing portraits hung on the walls. And the bar itself was set up pretty well, except for the glasses rack directly over the ice sink. As he looked it over, the kitchen door bumped open and a guy his own age came out with a tray of wineglasses. He set the tray down, gave Johnny a nod, and began slipping the glasses stem-first into the rack.

"Don't drop one," Johnny said.

The bartender shot him a look.

Johnny held up his hands. "I've been there, brother."

The bartender grinned. He knew what Johnny was saying: If you dropped a glass it would fall directly into the sink, and after you'd picked out the shards you'd have to replace all the ice. You'd scoop out what you could, and then you'd have to use buckets of hot water. And naturally this would only happen when you were deep in the weeds, with drink orders piled up and waitresses spitting nails.

"I'm guessing it's somebody's own design," Johnny said.

"Bingo." The barkeep carefully put the last glass away. "So how'd it go in there?"

"I learned that business was like war."

The bartender made a face. He reached into the cooler for a bottle of beer, levered the cap off, and set it in front of Johnny. "On him," he said. Then he took the cork-bottomed tray back to the kitchen.

Johnny watched little bubbles rise through the ale. He was supposed to be behaving himself. But Sarah was working at the Realty, the boys wouldn't be home for a couple of hours, and it would be rude to just walk out. It could even affect his job prospects. So he sat down and drank, which obliged him, when the bartender returned, to purchase another so he could leave a little something for a tip. The bartender was Navy—Johnny had seen the anchor tattoo when his sleeve had ridden up—and Johnny always tipped fellow vets.

"Will he mind me sitting here?" Johnny thought to ask.

"He's gone out. Got a big war council or something."

Johnny smiled and raised the beer. He'd almost finished it when Early Blake came in, saw his near-empty glass, and ordered him a refill. All right, Johnny thought, just one more, since it's him. But then you head home.

He asked Early how things were on the flats, and that led to stories about falling out of skiffs, stepping into honey pots, and dodging the clam cops. The bartender laughed and set them up again.

It was like a conspiracy, Johnny thought with awe.

The bartender did a magic trick involving ashtrays and shot glasses, and then Early related how when he was a young fellow he'd run up the river on a foggy day to steal an outboard from a guy who'd owed him for ten pecks of clams for over a year. The deadbeat had had a second outboard, though, and he'd come after Early and actually fired a couple of rounds at him through the murk. Early had to lie low in Preacher's Cove until the guy gave up.

It was a long, well-told tale, and by the time it was over they'd switched to Bacardi, but Johnny was careful to dilute each drink by eating the ice at the bottom of the glass. He forgot to keep track of the time, though, and later when Early looked at his watch and said, "Lord Almighty, how'd it get to be five o'clock?" Johnny was shocked.

Then he remembered the school bus and his kids.

"Yikes," he said, and got to his feet.

Early Blake laughed. "Somebody's in trouble."

"You don't know the half of it."

Outside Johnny looked in disbelief at the lowering sun. He'd wondered en route to the door about walking home—it wasn't far, and he wouldn't have to worry about running into Chief Foss, who was always willing to pull him over—but now he dismissed that idea. He just couldn't afford the time. Also, he'd have to explain why he hadn't driven. And there was one other reason: In Baxter people would stop and offer you a ride, and if that happened it would get around that he'd been drinking again.

So he threw his lanky frame over the bike, jammed three pieces of Juicy Fruit into his mouth, and pulled gently out into the street. He rode past the big Main Street flagpole and leaned around the corner to head slowly down Knox, past the Baptist Church with its high, white steeple and wide, groomed lawn. When he reached the bottom of the hill he was close enough to home to stop worrying about Chief Foss, but that only took his mind back to Sarah. A cold lump formed in his stomach, as if all the Bacardi-flavored ice were somehow reconstituting itself, and he wondered what he was going to tell her this time. He'd already worked late, had a flat tire, met an old friend. He wished to hell he could still joke his way out of trouble.

He'd been pretty good at that once upon a time. Inspired, even. Once he'd claimed to be an extraterrestrial, stranded on Earth, unable to understand the earthling concept of time. It had been a reference to a bad movie they'd taken the kids to see at the Baxter drive-in, called *Mordak from Mars.*

"Mordak sorry!" he'd said, circling Sarah with exaggerated, heavy-gravity steps, his imitation so dead-on that finally she'd had to smirk despite herself.

Afterward he'd used the routine shamelessly, and eventually it became a family joke. He and the kids would walk like Martians, chanting, "We come in peace!" as they followed Sarah around the house.

Or they'd be heading to Portland to visit Sarah's parents and to pass the time he'd tell them Mordak stories. One trip he told them about his escape to Earth in a ship fueled by astro-poop, and the boys made faces from their seats in the back and kicked their feet and said, *"Daaaad!"* Then he told them how he'd spent 146 years hiding out on the moon, spying down on Earth, looking for the perfect mate, and how he'd finally found their mom.

"Lucky me, huh?" Sarah had said.

There'd been a little something in her voice, because it hadn't been all that long since he'd come home at two in the morning with blood on his knuckles—sometimes he made a *lousy* human being—but he'd ignored it and pressed on.

"Mordak happy now!" he'd exclaimed, and they had rolled down Route 1, through small towns, past hayfields, and into stretches of pine woods, and he'd kept at it until everyone in the car was snickering helplessly.

Johnny squeezed the clutch and coasted quietly down Water Street, wobbling slightly. It was early spring, and the water black and high as it swept through the town and curved toward the bay, carrying bits of broken light from tall streetlights. Their house sat on a high bank looking across the street at the harbor, and for a moment, riding up the driveway, the house dark and still, he was frightened that Sarah had taken the kids and left, as she'd threatened to do more than once. Then he saw light in the kitchen.

Popping the clutch, he putted around the wagon, heeled down the kickstand, swung off the bike. He spat his wad of gum into the garden to the left of the door, where Sarah's poppies, closed up with evening, sat blindly at the end of their long necks. He took a deep breath and opened the door.

Sarah was standing at the kitchen sink, hand-washing her plate. Her back stiffened as Johnny clicked the door shut. His son Alec looked at him from the table, a book in one hand and his fork in the other.

"Hey, Smart Alec," Johnny said.

"You're home," Alec said.

Sarah turned then and gave him a look. Johnny admired the way her fair hair shone under the ceiling light. He thought she was pretty as anything, and wanted to kiss her and beg forgiveness, but that was another thing he'd done too often. Instead he gave her what he hoped was a chipper smile.

"I might have found something," he said. "Alva Potter needs a bartender. I filled out an application and he gave me an interview on the spot." He tried to breathe shallowly and not slur. But then the house tilted suddenly and he had to put a hand to the wall.

Sarah dropped her dishcloth and stalked out.

Johnny pushed off the wall and looked at his younger son. The ice in his gut grew edges and spires.

"Eric got sent home from school," Alec said.

"How come?" Johnny said.

"He got in another fight."

"Perfect," Johnny said. He reached to ruffle Alec's shaggy hair, but Alec raised the book to ward him off, so he said, "Sorry" and went into the living room, where Sarah sat with the newspaper, collapsing it to turn the pages in a kind of controlled fury.

Johnny told her he was sorry he'd come home late, but Potter had asked if he could buy him a beer after the interview, and he'd thought it wise to accept.

"What time was that, Johnny?"

"I didn't notice."

She crumpled the paper, turned the page.

"We really didn't drink that much. Mostly just talked about the job."

"Go look in the mirror," Sarah said.

They had a long, framed mirror on the wall above the register in the little hallway that led to the front door. Johnny walked over and took a look. A tired and haggard man stared back at him. Okay, he thought.

Back in the living room he said, "I guess I did it again."

Sarah closed the newspaper, captured a page.

"I'm sorry," Johnny said. "I should have been here."

"But you weren't," she said.

"I'll go up and see him."

"Better chew some more gum."

Johnny walked over to the stairway, jogged up the stairs. He ducked into the bathroom to brush his teeth, then knocked on Eric's door. After a moment, he pushed it open. Eric was sitting on his bed, facing the window in the dark. Johnny shuffled over and sat beside him.

He felt the bedspread under his hands, the little-kid quilt that Eric still used with its bright yellow stars, moons, and planets. Johnny remembered picking it out and missed the boy Eric had been in those days. He could always jostle him out of his moods back then. All he had to do was swoop down on him, crying, "Martian death match!," and Eric would try to run, but Johnny would catch him and sling him up on his shoulder and spin him around. Finally Eric would laugh despite himself and say, "Stop! I give!" and then he'd be happy, at least for a spell.

"Don't you want any dinner?" Johnny said now.

Eric shook his head, hid his face in the pillow.

Johnny looked at him helplessly. Then he said, "Heck with it—eating's for earthlings."

Eric didn't move or speak.

"Martians don't need to eat," Johnny went on. "Martians just synthesize nutrients out of the air. Of course it takes some concentration, and I've been living on Earth for quite a while; I've gotten used to eating, so maybe it isn't as easy as it once was, and I suppose if I wait too long there's the danger I might forget altogether . . ."

"Shut up, Dad," Eric said into the pillow.

Johnny shut up. Outside, cars ripped past their driveway and shot around the corner out of sight. The Baxter Speedway, they called it, because everybody from the far side of the river used their street to cut up to Route 1. They crossed the iron bridge to Water Street, hung a right, and were off to the races.

Eric sat up, face in his hands.

Johnny looked at his incongruously black hair—everybody else's was some variation of hay-colored—and his lean arms and said, "They pestering you at school again?" This was the third fight he'd heard about, and Eric had also been kicked out for a week for swearing at the principal.

Eric clenched his fists as if holding onto himself, tight. Then he jumped up, grabbed his jacket off the bedpost, and took off down the stairs.

Johnny listened to him run out of the house and slam the door and run down the driveway.

Then he fell back on the bed and looked up at the ceiling.

When Johnny walked into the living room, Sarah hadn't moved. Alec came out of the kitchen with a heaping bowl of ice cream and a glass of milk, the book tucked under his arm. He looked sideways at Johnny and went on up the stairway to his room opposite Eric's. In a moment the ceiling began to vibrate.

Johnny grinned weakly at Sarah. "He calls it music."

Sarah got purposefully to her feet and marched down to their bedroom off the front hallway. Johnny went back into the kitchen and looked at the chicken and the bowl of peas and the mashed potatoes. None of it was very appetizing. He might as well have been a real Martian, for all the effect that food had on him.

He looked at his jacket, hanging beside the door.

It had rained the day before and Johnny could see footprints in the mud. Eric had run all the way down past the mom-and-pop at the corner, and then the impressions changed; now he was walking.

Johnny imagined ducking into the store and grabbing a beer before continuing the search. But even *he* couldn't be that much of a loser. He didn't need it, anyway; he was still stepping on his own feet. He tracked Eric by streetlight onto the pedestrian footbridge and looked down at the fast swell of the water, the bridge strung sturdily to the other side. He started across, scanning for signs of his son on the opposite bank. Nothing there.

He turned to walk back, a little worried now; kids had drowned in the Baxter River before.

He'd almost reached Water Street when he heard the sob. It came again from somewhere low, and he peered over the railing to see his son sitting on a cross-girder, with his back against one of the posts that went down into the cement footings of the bridge. Eric had his head in his hands and the bridge arced over him and the water eddied noisily past just a few feet away.

Johnny backed off as quietly as he could. Then he tiptoed off the bridge, counted to ten, and stomped back, clapping his hands and howling an old Martian ditty he'd sung to Eric and his brother many times:

Mr. Mordak came to Earth,
From the planet of his birth,
Full of beauty, brains, and grace
Hoping to improve the race!

Eric appeared then, climbing lightly over the railing onto the footbridge. He didn't look at Johnny, just stood there with his head down and his hands in his jacket pockets.

Johnny said, "Second verse!"

"You can stop," Eric said. "I'll come back."

"Killjoy," Johnny said. "You've never accepted your Martian blood."

"Just shut up, Dad."

They started back to the house. When they turned onto Water Street it was quiet enough to hear the streetlight buzzing at the corner.

Eric still had his head down and his hands in his pockets. As they walked silently along, the river came up close and danced along under the streetlights and then shied away again.

"That's a good spot," Johnny said, finally.

Eric kicked at the mud without breaking stride.

"When I was your age," Johnny said, "I'd hide under the front porch."

He remembered ducking behind the rain barrel, crawling over the damp soil, huddling next to the foundation while his father stomped around the house, muttering angrily. He remembered praying for angels to come, something that he'd learned in Sunday school might be possible.

"So why were you hiding?" Eric said after a moment.

"Oh, the old man," Johnny said. "He'd get drinking. Sometimes he was a little mean."

"My grandfather?"

"Technically speaking," Johnny said.

They walked another few steps.

"Well," Eric said, "at least you're not mean."

It took a moment for Eric's words to sink in. But then they fell straight through Johnny and smashed on the ice. He felt it like glass as they trudged past close-set homes with dark windows and the pale light of TVs, past the machine shop with the ham radio antenna on its roof. Nothing came to mind that he might say, and they followed the river silently to the end of the block, stopping diagonally across from their driveway.

When the downstairs lights winked on, Eric took a step into the street, as if it had been some kind of signal. But at that same moment a pickup thumped off the bridge, skidding their way, and Johnny quickly grabbed his son and pulled him back. The truck rushed furiously up, fishtailing on the wet pavement, straightening then and rushing by so close they had to pinch back against the guardrail. The pickup slid out of sight around a curve, tires squawking, and Johnny held his breath, dreading a crash.

He was on the town ambulance crew, drafted because he'd been a recon medic, and it would be his duty to run and try to help them. But nothing happened; the pickup just kept speeding along, headlights leading the way out of the curve and off down the street—and finally Johnny let himself exhale. Then he felt Eric shiver.

He drew him in closer. "You all right, kiddo?"

"Uh-huh," Eric said. But he shivered again.

"It can be scary, can't it?" Johnny said. "This old planet of yours."

There was another loud squeal from far down the street.

"Who says it's my planet?" Eric said then.

Johnny would have given anything at that moment to be able to say exactly the right thing, but he hadn't been doing so well in that department. Also, he was afraid his voice would crack, and then Eric might spook and try to squirm free. Johnny couldn't stand the thought of that.

He held on and looked toward the bridge. It was all clear, and he checked the other way, where the speeding truck had gone. That was all right, too. He knew he was stalling, but still couldn't trust himself to speak. Then Eric started to fidget, and it felt like the last desperate moment when Johnny finally thought of something that he *could* do.

It had to be better than nothing, right?

What he could do was lean away from his son, as if he were only taking one more look at the street. Eric would be paying attention—kids always paid attention—and Johnny could cock his head left and right, ever so nonchalant, smiling innocently . . . and then suddenly take off! Yes, he could run with lots of arm motion, but not really that fast! He could run just slowly enough so that a boy could catch up.

Boys were like dogs: They couldn't resist a chase. And when Eric pulled even, why, they could turn on the jets. Johnny could practically see it. They could run as fast as any two earthlings, straight across the Baxter Speedway, zooming up the bank toward the well-lighted house.

Early

I never had any trouble getting up in the morning, and was usually the first one out on the flats. That's why everyone called me Early instead of Earl, which was my real name. But when I lost my Evangeline I seemed to lose all my ambition, too. I'd lie awake all hours and then morning would come and I'd feel ninety years old.

Finally my daughter-in-law got fed up.

"Life goes on, Early!" Dinah said, among a few other things.

She had that right—hadn't she lost Earl Jr. at Normandy?—and she kept at me until eventually it sank in.

One morning I heard the foghorns, and that's all it took. I remembered I'd been looking for the right tide and weather, and I hauled out of bed, figuring it was time to go and make myself some money.

I guess it was about three thirty. We only had one boarder at that time—Frank Stover was his name—and Dinah had put him in the corner room opposite the river, so I was pretty sure I wouldn't wake him. Not that he'd give a damn about me going out poaching; Frank Stover wasn't above sneaking around some himself. It was just that he did a lot of driving, and when he took a day off he liked to catch up on his sleep.

I went down the stairs and fed the fire in the kitchen stove from the basket of sticks young James kept filled in the corner. I let the coffeepot heat up to a boil and filled my vacuum bottle that was a present from Vangie the Christmas before she got sick. It was to keep me warm when she couldn't do it herself. I held the bottle against my cheek, then grabbed a handful of hard-boiled eggs out of the icebox, and went out the door past the chicken coop.

The foghorns were still blowing down the bay and the stuff was so thick I could feel it on my face. I walked past Frank Stover's Rambler and my old truck and on down the path to the rickety dock Primus had built thirty years before. I'd been after James for some time to shore it up, but so far he hadn't listened. But he was a teenager with no daddy, and you had to allow.

I took care where the planks were missing and went down to the outboard and got in. There were the usual clunky sounds of moving around in a boat, but the fog muffled it so there wasn't noise enough to wake anybody. My boots and rubber gloves and rollers and rake were already in the boat, and I cast her off and paddled out slow and quiet into the river.

Man, it was some thick of fog. The tide was just starting to turn and there was plenty of water. I let myself drift down below the house a ways, then pulled on the outboard a couple of times, and she fired up. I leaned her out until she ran smooth. Paddling out I'd heard some kind of fish rising, just popping the surface, and once I got going I put a line over the side with a dried-up old worm on the hook, but nothing bit, and I went on up the river.

A ways along a boat passed me going the other direction, but I never saw him. Sounded like a lobster boat, though, or maybe a warden. They ran the same kind of boat, and they liked to go out in the fog.

If it was a warden he was probably on his way down to where all the pot buoys were, where it got saltier down near the bay. In years past I might've turned back anyway, but it seemed to have gotten harder to change my mind once I was set on something, and I was set on Preacher's Cove. It had been off limits for a while now, and I'd been saving it for the right day.

I could picture all those clams waiting in the mud. I could see myself pulling in a boatload of steamers and making a week's pay in one night. I could damn sure use the money. It wasn't easy getting by this time of year. Or any other time, for that matter. You did a little of this and a little of that. Took in boarders. Redcapped at the train station. Hired out to work the hayfields or pick cabbage for the sauerkraut farm. Dug clams, mostly, which no one had done in Preacher's Cove for near two years. At first it had been the red tide; then afterward they'd decided to keep it closed, because they could. They said the clam population needed it, but I had my doubts. It seemed to me there were as many clams around as there ever were.

It took me near an hour to run upriver to town. I swung in close to where I could see the pier and the new streetlights, the ones that looked like old-time oil lanterns, then went back out and under the bridge and up to where the river hooked north. The water was ripping through here now, and it was slow going with my twelve-horse. It was almost five o'clock, still an hour from sunrise, and still foggy as hell.

I ran over near the east side so I wouldn't miss where the bank broke away. The water had dropped a foot or so; you could tell from the wet marks on the rocks. When the break came I throttled down and went real slow into the cove. There was a place I knew about just inside where the bushes grew down, where you could hide a small boat. I took one turn around to look things over and it was all clear so I went in there and cut my power. I swung the prop up and let the boat drift forward and I grabbed the bushes and hauled myself in. A branch snatched my cap off but I caught it before it got wet. I stepped into my boots and got out into the water and tied her up.

I couldn't see well enough yet to pull the clams by hand the way I liked to in soft mud, so I took the rake and two of the rollers and walked around through the bushes to the head of the cove, where the mud was just starting to show. I was moving quiet as I could in the dark, so I heard it without any trouble when somebody whistled soft from the trees.

I listened to see if it would come again and it did, so low this time I could barely hear it. I thought about running, then laughed at myself and carried my gear on over. A clam cop wouldn't whistle.

There was an old homestead foundation over there, just a hole lined with rocks, and a dirt road that came in through the woods. When I got to the foundation a tall, blond man stepped out from behind one of the big pines and I saw it was Johnny Lunden. There were a couple rollers and a clam rake on the ground where he'd been hiding. I knew he'd been digging again since he'd lost his bartending job. I'd seen him out on the river, waved at him going by, but I never figured him for a poacher. I guess it didn't seem like his kind of trouble.

"Early Blake," he said. "You better not be sneaking up on me."

I laughed because of the serious look on his face.

"I'm glad you think something's funny," he said.

"Lots of things are funny, Mr. Lunden."

"Oh, don't I know it, Mr. Blake."

We liked to call each other "mister" for a joke, see.

"You do know these flats are closed?"

"Just on my way around to the river."

"Well, ain't that a coincidence!" He put his hands on his hips and cocked his head over. He always could make me laugh ever since he was a little towheaded kid and would come downriver and play with Earl Jr. He was always just lively and comical like that. Which you wouldn't have expected with all he had going on at home, with those parents he was blessed with.

He grabbed his gear and we walked back to the cove.

Then we started right in, driving the rakes into the mud, sifting around for clams, loading up our rollers. We worked in a long curve along near the shore and were halfway to the river when he said, "I was awful sorry to hear about Evangeline."

I just kept working my rake. I didn't like talking about her. Just thinking about her I could imagine she was listening, but it didn't work when somebody else was involved.

Johnny didn't say anything more and we kept working until the rollers were full, then walked over to the water and rocked them so the clams circled up and around—that's why they're called rollers, see—and got rinsed off. We carried them back to shore, over to the side where I'd hidden my boat. A full roller weighs about forty pounds, and with one in each hand we were breathing pretty hard by the time we set them down.

Johnny looked at our footprints leading around the cove.

"Probably should have started the other way," he said. So he could have ended up by where he'd come in, he meant.

"I'll take you up the river when we're done; you can cut through from there."

"That'll work," he said.

We sat down to take a breather and Johnny offered me a smoke. I offered him some coffee back, and a hard-boiled egg, but he said no thanks. He blew out smoke like a sigh and drew his legs up and put his elbows on his knees. He took another drag and stared out at the fog and for a second he looked pretty sad. I guess he was thinking about some things. Then he realized I was watching and he put the wise-guy grin back on, the way it generally was.

"I heard you had some hard luck, too," I said.

The story was that his wife had run off with her boss and taken the kids with her, and I decided I should mention it because he'd been kind enough to speak of Evangeline. He was all right, Johnny Lunden was, and I felt for him. Like I said, he'd been friends with Earl Jr. growing up, and later on one of his own boys was tight with young James, and Johnny used to come down to the farm and pick James up and take them all to the drive-in.

Then I used to go up to the Neutral Corner for the Friday-night fights after they put the television set in, and when Johnny was bartending he always treated me good. I never had that feeling he'd be nice to my face and call me names behind my back, like some folks would. He'd slip me a beer now and then, too.

"Hard luck," he said now. "I guess I did, but it was my own fault."

"Well, I was sorry to hear it, anyway."

He took a last drag on the cigarette and snapped it off into the bushes. I capped my vacuum bottle and we took a couple more rollers each back to the mud. We started where we'd left off and went back the other way. The sun was up and everything was brighter; we followed our own footprints around the cove, working without our rakes now that we could see good enough to find the little holes the clams make when they suck the water in.

We'd swing the rollers ahead, step up beside them, dig as many out as we could reach. Then we'd move up again. There's a rhythm you get into and it makes the time go. We worked all the way across and started back, and we weren't talking and I was starting to feel a little dreamy, what with the short night and the rhythm of working. Vangie was back in my head, too, although a little sideways of where she usually was.

We filled the rollers, rinsed them, and took them back and sat down for another cigarette. Johnny leaned sideways and pulled a little silver flask out of his hip pocket and offered it to me. It ruins me to drink in the morning, but he went ahead and helped himself and kept at it pretty steady. He'd hold the flask to his mouth and sort of flip up the tail end. Then he'd take a drag off the butt and bring the flask up again. When we went back out it didn't seem to slow him down or affect him much, except he got a little more talkative.

Maybe the fog helped, too, in that regard. It was still thick as hell—you couldn't see twenty feet ahead—so it was like we were the only people in the world. He laughed and told me how he couldn't figure himself out sometimes, why he drank so much and got in fistfights and chased after girls who weren't worth half of what he had at home.

"Or used to have," he said.

He said it'd been like this since he came home. He'd go along all right but something would just set him off. Everything would start to get tight around him and he'd have to do something to loosen it up. Then he looked at me like he expected me to come up with an explanation, but I didn't have anything useful to say. I could remember some things I'd done, too, when I was married to about the best girl in the world.

It wasn't more than a half hour after that when we heard the boat coming up the rip. The current was such that they had to pour on the coal, and that made them pretty loud. It sounded like it was maybe the same boat I'd heard before, and after I told Johnny we took off at a sloppy kind of gallop back across the mud.

We sloshed through shallow water up to the bushes and set the rollers into the boat. Then we got in too and listened as the other guy worked closer. Sure enough, they came right into the cove. I caught a shadow of them passing by. There was still enough water and it was still foggy enough that they had to ride a ways in to see if anyone had been poaching, and as soon as they were clear of us we took our chance. There wasn't any way they could hear us scratching through the bushes over their motor, so we pulled on the branches and slid out and hugged close to the bank until we were in the river.

I paddled us out into the current and let it take us down toward the hook. We picked up speed and a half mile from the cove I fired up the outboard and we took off downstream at a pretty good clip. I might have waited longer, I suppose. Anyway, about ten seconds later I heard them torque up and come right along after us. I hoped we had enough of a head start. If we could get to Baxter, we could just tie up at the landing and hide somewhere. Then after a while we could reappear and they'd have no proof we'd been doing anything wrong. Hiding along the river was out, because the tide had shrunk back enough so that we couldn't get to shore. There were a couple of long docks, but I was pretty sure they'd check them out. So we raced around the hook and started down the stretch toward the bridge, and it was right there that the outboard up and quit.

"What are we doing?" Johnny Lunden said.

"Ain't doing nothing," I said. "She just died."

"Perfect," he said.

We could hear the clam cops swerving back and forth in the channel in case we might try to sit still in the fog and let them go by. Which was good, because it gave us some extra time. I told Johnny to dump the steamers while I went to work on the motor. I'd been hoping to save our payday, but it didn't make sense anymore.

"You sure?" he said.

I didn't even bother answering, and he got to work on it.

Sometimes those Johnsons when you ran them hard would vacuum-lock, and I was hoping that was the case. Meanwhile, we were still riding the current toward the bridge, swinging sideways like a piece of driftwood. The clam cops were roaring along after us, tacking back and forth. I took my gloves off and loosened the vent screw to let some air in. Then I pumped the primer bulb fast as I could until it was hard as a rock. I looked at Johnny and said, "Here goes nothing," and pulled the cord.

Nothing is exactly what happened, and he said, "Uh-oh."

But I went through the routine again, and then the third time she coughed and started.

"Praise the Lord!" Johnny Lunden said.

I straightened us out and ran it full bore. We could hear the other boat gaining, but I'd got us going in time, and we shot under the bridge and over to Baxter Landing.

We had tied up at the float and run up on the pier by the time they came by. We sat with our backs to somebody's pickup while they swung over to check out the landing and throttled back enough so we could hear them talking.

"I bet that's them right there," one of them said. "That one, full of rollers."

"Wouldn't be surprised," the other one said.

"Want me to check the motor, see if it's warm?"

"Naw, they're long gone. It would just make me feel bad."

The first one laughed and they throttled up again and peeled away from the float and turned upriver, I guess to make sure they hadn't missed us on the way down. As soon as it sounded like they were on the other side of the bridge, we walked down the gangway.

I asked Johnny if he wanted to come along and have a bite to eat—told him I'd drive him back afterward. But he said no thanks, he had to figure out how he was going to get back to pick up the truck he'd borrowed before it got impounded or something.

I helped him carry his rollers and rake up onto the pier and we set them aside where he could leave them for the time being. He took his flask out, turned it upside down and shook it, but nothing came out. He laughed and stuck it back in his pocket.

"Wish we hadn't dumped everything," he said.

"Me too."

"Guess we had to."

"No way around it."

He stuck out his hand and said, "It's been a pleasure doing business with you, Mr. Blake," and then he set off up the hill toward the street. I went back down to the boat and this time I let her drift a good ways before I started her up again. The fog hung like a shroud over the river all the way back, and it was quiet as a church.

Frank Stover was sitting on the end of my dock fishing when I got home. I threw him the painter and he stood up and pulled me alongside and tied the line off. I climbed up and said, "Thank you kindly."

"My pleasure, Early," he said, and looked into the boat. "I don't see any steamers."

"Didn't work out," I said. "You catch any fish?"

"Drowned a few worms, is all."

You could still hear the foghorns downriver. I left my gear in the boat and headed up the dock. Frank followed me with his fishing pole over his shoulder. We took long steps over the missing boards, then walked up the path past his Rambler. I looked in at the stuff he carted up and down the coast.

"I was really hoping for some steamers," Frank said.

"Dinah will fix you a good hot lunch."

He made some other comment, but I didn't hear what it was because after saying that about something hot, I remembered my vacuum bottle. I'd forgotten all about it, and didn't have it with me. I couldn't recall seeing it on the trip back. Of course, I'd been pretty busy, but usually it sat right up against the transom.

I tried to remember if I'd thought to grab it when we were lifting the rollers in. Maybe I did, but Johnny or I could have knocked it overboard while we were scrambling around. Or one of those branches might have caught it somehow. It bothered me I couldn't remember. All I had to do was look in the boat, of course, but I stood there listening to the foghorns and Frank Stover grumbling about steamers instead.

I was pretty sure it was gone, probably still bobbing along in the Baxter. That vacuum bottle was tight, and might float all the way down to the bay. Maybe then the tide would wash it back in. I pictured it going back and forth for who knows how long, and eventually somebody finding it in the seaweed. They'd see the sun shining off it and they'd open it up and there'd be a whiff of old coffee. They'd rinse it in the surf, then take it on home. I imagine they'd feel pretty lucky.

Tomi

It was the Fourth of July and Tomi Lambert had gone to bed with another of her growing pains. They were mysterious and always seemed to show up at the worst times. Like today, with a parade in the offing. There was nothing to do but grin and bear it, according to her mother. They never lasted all that long and eventually would go away altogether; meanwhile, some more fun stuff would come around.

Her mother had laughed, saying this. It was all part of becoming a woman, she'd said.

"Then I think I'll stay a girl!" Tomi had said.

"Oh, honey," her mother had said.

Tomi turned the pillow over and laid her head back down. She could hear her father rummaging around in the attic. After a while he came down the stepladder, and she went to the door and opened it a crack. He was wearing his Navy jacket. Tugging sharply at it, he marched to the stairwell and headed down to the kitchen.

Tomi slipped over to look. He was standing at attention in the kitchen doorway.

"Still fits," he said in his deep voice.

"Does that mean we're marching?" Tomi's mother said from the kitchen.

"Not if you don't want to," Tomi's father said.

"It's just getting into all that old gear."

Tomi's father went into the kitchen then, and Tomi scampered for the attic. You didn't get chances like this all the time. She climbed the stepladder and squirmed through the hatch. The attic was lit by a bare bulb, and between the floor joists was insulation that looked like pink cotton candy. Tomi knew if you stepped on it, you'd go right through. That was one reason the attic was supposed to be off limits. There was also rat poison and exposed nails and other perils her parents had only hinted at. But a plank led across the joists to a plywood floor, and over there it didn't look dangerous—just interesting. There were bulky shapes covered with sheets. Clothing hung from a wooden rod next to a jumbled stack of cartons.

Tomi walked across the plank, arms out for balance.

The first carton held only old bank statements and checkbooks. The next was full of black-and-white snapshots of people she didn't know. Then she tried a shoe box and inside found a small photo album. When she opened the album several folded papers fell out. She carefully opened one of them: a fragile newspaper clipping that turned out to be the obituary of one Philip Metcalf, an American RAF pilot who had been shot down over the Istrian peninsula on July 2, 1945.

Tomi didn't know what "RAF" meant, and she'd never heard of Philip Metcalf. She studied his grainy black-and-white picture and whispered *Istrian peninsula*. He'd given his all, the clipping said, and was sadly missed by mother Mary and father Henry of Portland, and by his bride, Susan O'Leary Metcalf, of Baxter. Philip and Susan had met in Portland while she was in training to become a

US Army nurse, and had only been married a week before Lieutenant Metcalf was deployed overseas.

Wait a minute, Tomi thought: Susan O'Leary was her mother!

She dug into the rest of the loose material, found more wartime newspaper stories, several notes from the Red Cross, and a letter from His Majesty, King George VI, extending the Crown's sympathy for the enormous loss Mrs. Metcalf had suffered for the cause of liberty and freedom.

A *king* had written to her mother!

Tomi kept digging. The album contained wedding pictures of Philip Metcalf and Tomi's mother in their military uniforms. They were feeding each other cake; they were part of a group of others in uniform, holding drinks and laughing. They were waltzing cheek to cheek, then dancing fast.

Cutting a rug, Tomi thought. She knew you could call it that because she'd been hiding under the kitchen table one morning when her mother had grabbed her father's hands and had said, "Come on, old man, let's cut a rug!" But Tomi's father wouldn't cooperate and finally she'd let go. He didn't like to dance anymore because of his leg, Tomi's mother told her later. Men were sensitive like that sometimes. Philip Metcalf liked to dance, though; the pictures showed him in such lively poses—crouched and corkscrewed, grinning widely—that Tomi could tell he was enjoying every moment.

Tomi heard her father start back up the stairs. He always made them creak, and didn't move very fast, so there was plenty of time to hotfoot it back to the hatch and pose innocently on the stepladder, as if she'd only been *thinking* about sneaking into the attic.

"Get down from there, Tomasina," her father said.

"Yes, Daddy," Tomi said in her good-girl voice.

She backed down the stepladder. "What are all those boxes, anyway?"

"That's your mother's stuff."

He started up the ladder, still wearing his Navy jacket.

Tomi knew he'd been in the war, too; that's what had happened to his leg. He'd been through a lot, her mother had said. His ship had been torpedoed, and he'd hidden in the jungle and eaten grubs and worms to survive. Tomi sort of liked those stories even if they were disgusting. The only one she didn't like was how he was finally caught and locked in a big, dark box and mistreated horribly, but that one led to her all-time favorite: how he'd met up with her mother in the hospital after he was rescued. Her mother had been stationed on Tinian, which is where they'd taken him to recuperate. He'd been very sick and hurt, and she'd helped to make him well. Once Tomi's father had said that when he'd come out of his fever to see a girl from his own hometown standing there, he'd thought at first she was some kind of an angel.

"God forbid!" Tomi's mother had said, laughing.

When her father went back downstairs, Tomi considered going up to the attic again. But her legs still hurt, so she went back to bed instead. She didn't want to miss the parade because of a stupid growing pain.

She looked at the ceiling and thought about Philip Metcalf. It was too bad *he* couldn't have swum to an island. Maybe her mother could have helped *him* get well. Tomi imagined him in a hospital bed, looking up at her angelic mother, and suddenly the grainy newspaper image came to life in her mind and it was almost as if he were right there in the room. She could sense his tousled hair and whiskery cheeks and broad shoulders. It was a little scary, but she liked it, too, because he seemed nice, and when her father knocked on her door to say it was time for the parade, she was sorry that it made Philip Metcalf disappear.

Tomi's parents were quiet in the car, but they didn't talk much anyway if she was around. She had to hide in the coat closet to hear anything good. From the closet she'd learned that Father Daley was getting a little long in the tooth—she liked imagining *that*—and that Alva Potter had been a draft dodger. She heard other good stuff, too, like how they might have another baby before too long, and how her Grandpa Lambert had shot a moose in his backyard and then had had to pay a fine. But other times they would lower their voices, and then Tomi would know she was missing out. Once her mother came out of the kitchen crying, and Tomi hadn't heard enough to know any reason why.

Mr. Lambert parked at the high school. Tomi said good-bye and skipped down to Main Street. She trotted past people on the sidewalk and sitting on folding chairs in their yards. When she passed the Mitchell family, her friend Julie waved, but Julie's cousin Arnold was there, too, standing a little aside, and Tomi couldn't stand Arnold, who was a bully, so she ran on. She saw old Primus Blake and his family, all sitting on the library steps. James Blake was nicer than most older kids—he'd always smile and say hi—but his mother, Dinah, was loud and scared her a little, so she didn't stop here, either. She kept going past hot dog carts and cotton candy stands and balloon vendors. The balloons reminded her of Philip Metcalf, the way he'd sort of bobbed around in her room.

Finally she saw Johnny Lunden standing by the monument, and thought he'd be a good one to watch with. He'd grown up with her parents and sometimes he worked for the town, sweeping or shoveling the sidewalks, picking up trash beside the roads.

He lived over the hardware store, and when they were in town they'd see him sitting by his window, watching everybody, waving now and then, and sometimes when they were ready to leave he would come down and lean on the car and talk. He always included Tomi, and she liked that. She liked the eagle on his arm and his straw-colored mustache and the way he always joked about everything.

When Tomi skipped up now he cocked his head and said, "Well, dog my cats, if it isn't Miss Tomi-salami!"

Tomi giggled. "Can I watch with you, Mr. Lunden?"

"It would be a rare honor," Johnny Lunden said.

Tomi sat on the base of the statue of the soldier holding a rifle. She made sure to tuck her dress down to hide her underpants, the way her mother had taught her. Otherwise boys like Arnold Stimpson or Daryl Sleeper or that Lucas Hurd would try to look. She peered between her knees at her sneakers, then looked up at Johnny Lunden.

"How come you're not in the parade?"

"Oh, goodness." He lowered a small, flat bottle.

Tomi's eyes narrowed. "Wouldn't they let you?"

"Good grief," he said. "They practically begged me."

"Why didn't you, then?"

"If I did, then who would you watch with?" he said with a grin.

Tomi frowned, thinking that one over. Then she heard the high school band start up. She couldn't see them yet. It sounded like the instruments weren't quite in tune. She took clarinet lessons, and she could tell. The drums were good, though, rattling and thumping. She liked the bass drum especially, its deep boom as much a feeling as a sound.

"Mr. Lunden?" Tomi was still watching for the parade. "Do you know who Philip Metcalf was? He was married to my mom. They were only married a week before he went away."

"Where did you hear that, honey?"

"I found out by myself."

"Well," Johnny Lunden said, "it was a long time ago."

"They used to cut a rug!" Tomi said.

"Oh, yes," he smiled. "They most certainly did."

"Then they shot him down in the war."

Johnny Lunden frowned and raised the flat bottle. Tomi watched him closely. She knew he was a drinker. Her parents had talked about him in the kitchen. Her father had said, "I don't know why you give him the time of day," and her mother had said, "Because we were friends, Roger," and her father had said, "Ancient history." But Johnny Lunden still seemed like a friend to Tomi. He was always so nice. When Grandpa Lambert fell down the steps at their house, he was one of the men who came in the ambulance. Johnny Lunden saw her looking and lowered the bottle.

"Old Tomi-salami," he said.

The parade came steadily into range. Two fire trucks were first, lights blinking and sirens so loud that Tomi had to plug her ears. Then the high school band, led by a man walking backwards. Next the veterans, with Tomi's mother striding smoothly and Tomi's father limping hard to keep up. Tomi waved, but knew they weren't allowed to wave back.

Behind the veterans were floats, with kids self-importantly slinging candy, then the town band, sitting in folding chairs on a flatbed trailer. When the trailer pulled abreast, Tomi said good-bye to Johnny Lunden.

"Good-bye, honey," he said back.

She hurried to catch up to her parents and stayed alongside them past the town hall and through iron gates into the town cemetery, where there were little American flags on many of the graves. The parade stopped there and Father Daley said a prayer for the sons and daughters of Baxter who had made the ultimate sacrifice. He read a list of names, and Philip Metcalf wasn't on it because he was from Portland, but Earl Blake Jr. was.

After the prayer someone played "Taps," and three of the veterans wearing bright white gloves raised rifles and fired into the air toward the river. Tomi could look down the hill behind the cemetery and see the boats sitting there. After the rifle shots the boats started their motors and rode away.

Everyone in the cemetery walked back to the town lawn, where there were horseshoe pits, pony rides, and barbecued chicken lunches served at long tables. Tomi and her parents didn't stay to eat, because they were going to the AMVETS supper later on, but as they wandered through the crowd she saw Johnny Lunden, sitting with three women and three men. He was laughing and waving a drumstick, and there was a balloon dancing from the back of his chair. Tomi stared until her mother said, "Don't be rude."

A little later they went home and she took a nap while her father drove to the airstrip that he'd cleared in the woods out by the old Captain Lambert cabin. He'd decided to go back to being a pilot a few years after he'd come home from the war, and had bought an airplane with a GI loan and started up the air taxi there. Today he had a trip to do, but it was just over to Portland, and he was sure he'd be back in time for the supper.

After the tables were cleared and they'd recited the Pledge of Allegiance, a band began playing at one end of the AMVETS hall. That brought many of the grown-ups onto the dance floor, snapping their fingers and nodding their heads. Tomi sat up straight, so no one would think she was tired. She didn't want to miss anything. She especially wouldn't have wanted to miss it when Johnny Lunden came in, laughing and going from table to table, shaking hands and slapping backs. She wouldn't have wanted to miss him cutting a rug with one lady after another, either.

All the ladies seemed to think it was fun.

After one dance Johnny looked around the room and his eyes settled on Tomi. When she waved he came walking over.

"Lieutenant?" he said to her father. "With your permission?"

Then he bowed to Tomi. "May I have the honor of this dance, Miss Tomi-salami?"

"I can't dance!" Tomi laughed.

"Of course you can," Johnny Lunden said.

Tomi looked at her mother, and when she said, "Go ahead, honey," she took Johnny's hand and let him lead her onto the dance floor. It made her nervous, but then he held both of her hands very gently and she felt better. When the music began he winked and said, "Just do what I do, kiddo." He made a cross-step, and repeated the move the other way. Tomi followed, watching his legs, but it was hard to imitate him exactly because he was so much taller. He showed her how to skip sideways, still holding hands, and how to let go of one hand and spin under the other one. Then he dropped his arms straight down and sort of jogged in place, jutting his chin forward and back. Tomi laughed too hard to do this very well, and he went back to the sideways skip, arranging it so that when the song ended, they were right back where they'd started.

Johnny pulled out Tomi's chair, then said, "One more favor, Lieutenant?" and held out a hand to her mother.

"Oh, Johnny," Tomi's mother laughed. "Haven't you had enough?"

"For old times' sake." Johnny Lunden looked at the stage and snapped his fingers. He twitched his shoulders, wagged his head. He grinned at Tomi's mother and said, "Come on, let's shake a leg. The lieutenant won't mind."

Tomi's mother looked helplessly at Tomi's father.

"Suit yourself," Tomi's father said.

Tomi's mother said, "All right, one dance!" and when Johnny Lunden started her toward the floor, she looked over her shoulder and said, "I'll be right back!"

Tomi's father gave a little wave.

Tomi sat up even straighter. Her mother and Johnny Lunden walked to the middle of the floor. Tomi's mother leaned back and looked at him. Then they started in dancing. Tomi's mother smiled with her chin up as he turned her to one side, pulled her back, and twirled her around.

Then they really took off. Tomi liked how he was all quick steps and slapping feet, but his head hardly moved at all. She liked how her mother had no trouble keeping up. Her mother was a great dancer! The two of them strutted and high-stepped and whirled until almost all the other dancers pulled back to give them extra room. Some even cheered and clapped. Only Alva Potter and his wife were able to keep up, and finally they stopped, too. When the song ended, Tomi's mother and Johnny Lunden stayed put, and it wasn't until three dances later that he finally brought her back to the table.

Tomi thought she looked very pretty with her face all flushed.

"You've still got it, Susie!" Johnny Lunden said. He winked at Tomi, formally saluted her father, and walked off, mopping his forehead with a handkerchief and stuffing it into his hip pocket. He walked all the way across the hall and then disappeared through a side door.

"Time for another drink," Tomi's father said.

"Don't be mean," Tomi's mother said. She was still catching her breath.

"Maybe he'll ask you to dance again."

"You said it was all right, honey."

"Not exactly," Tomi's father said.

When Johnny Lunden came back in through the same door a few minutes later, Tomi watched to see if he'd pick up where he'd left off, and wondered if he'd ask her to dance again. But this time he just sat at a table by himself and watched. A few dances later the band announced a break, and then Tomi's father shoved his chair back and said, "Are we ready?"

They got up and walked to the door under the red exit sign. During the ride home Tomi sat quietly in the backseat, watching her parents. But they kept their eyes on the road and didn't talk.

Tomi said good night, ran upstairs, and counted to fifty. Then she tiptoed back down and ducked into the coat closet. She opened the door a fraction to listen. Her father was doing most of the talking, but it was one of those times when Tomi couldn't quite hear. When he came out and marched up the stairs, though, she could tell he wasn't very happy.

She waited until he returned—in his bathrobe, now—and when the discussion resumed, she slipped out of the closet and stole upstairs herself. The stepladder was still in place, and in a flash she was back in the attic, looking for the photo with all the friends in uniform. She found it and—just as she'd thought—one of them was Johnny Lunden, standing next to Philip Metcalf, leaning on his shoulder with a big smile on his face. You could tell it was him, even without a mustache.

Tomi flipped to the dance photos. They were even better now that she'd actually seen her mother shake a leg. She imagined her mother dancing with Philip Metcalf the way she'd danced with Johnny Lunden, and the idea drew her in so deeply that when the stepladder rattled, it barely registered. Then it rattled again and Tomi knew suddenly it was her mother—too light to make the stairs creak—coming to put her nurse's uniform away.

Tomi put the top back on the shoe box and slipped over to hide behind the chimney. It was all she could think of to do. She made herself as small as possible and hunkered there against the wall, watching her mother climb through the hatch with the nurse's uniform over her arm.

Her mother stood under the bare bulb, then set off across the plank. On the other side she hooked her uniform up, stepped back, and clasped her hands in front of her. For a moment she stood still, looking at the uniforms. Then, so suddenly that Tomi caught her breath, she tipped her head, pivoted lightly, and began to dance, right there in the attic! She held one hand high and tucked the other around the waist of an invisible partner and twirled gracefully over the plywood, coming so close at one point that Tomi thought for sure she'd be discovered. But her mother only spiraled back the way she'd come, stopping in front of the uniforms again to curtsy.

Tomi's mother straightened and stood looking as before. Then she covered her face with her hands. Her shoulders trembled as if she might be crying, but in the weak light it was hard for Tomi to be sure.

Tomi kept an eye on her while carefully shifting position. She'd been dying to move, because her legs were hurting like the dickens again. Not just her legs, actually; it seemed to be spreading. She'd thought at first it was just another growing pain, showing up at exactly the wrong time, but now she was starting to wonder. She wondered if it might be that other stuff her mother had warned her about instead, that becoming-a-woman stuff. She certainly hoped that wasn't it, though.

Settled cross-legged now, watching her mother and aching in several new ways, Tomi didn't feel nearly ready to become a woman.

Mark

Mark Mitchell was fourteen, and not ordinarily one to volunteer for household chores, but on this day when his father went outside to smoke his pipe and the other four kids vamoosed into the living room, he lingered in the kitchen to help his mother clear the table. While she carried the big serving dish over, he stacked dirty plates and listened to the collies yip and howl from the dog pen. It always riled them up when someone went outside. The big boy collie they called Mr. Man usually started in, and that set the rest of them off.

When Mark carried the plates over, his mother looked at him in surprise.

"Why, thank you, Mark," she said.

Mark shrugged and lowered the plates into the sink.

"You're still my good boy." His mother tried to kiss his cheek, rolled her eyes when he ducked away. "Well, you are," she said, and scraped a plate into the dog pan on the counter.

At the table, Mark arranged eight glasses into two clusters and picked them up with his fingertips. When they clinked he looked at his mother. She'd heard it and was staring his way.

"Please don't carry them like that," his mother said.

Mark held the glasses out. "It's all right, see?"

"I asked you not to."

"But it's quicker." Mark walked carefully toward her.

"Mark!"

"I can't stop now." He lowered them safely into the sink and with his mother's eyes still on him, turned and walked with a sort of flinty dignity into the living room. All the good places there were occupied, as he'd known they would be. He'd counted on it, in fact. He sat on the floor near the box that held the latest litter, drew his knees up, and looked at Mindy with her six tugging and pushing puppies. Mindy was his mother's prize bitch.

"Good girl," he said, and patted her. She let her head back down and he touched the puppies. They were taut and hungry and squirmed under his hand.

"I beat you!" his little brother Ricky taunted from the couch, where he was squeezed against the near arm by Linda and Julie.

"I let you," Mark said coolly.

"Did not!"

"Shut up."

"That's enough," Mark's father said from the doorway. He came walking in, the smell of pipe smoke clinging to his flannel shirt. "Any more bickering and we'll just leave the TV off."

"No!" the kids on the couch cried.

"Mark?"

"I'm sorry."

"All right, then." Mark's father looked into the hallway. "Lois?"

Mark's mother came in, wiping her hands on her apron, giving Mark a look that meant she was still put out. Mark's father switched the light off—the room going dusky—and turned the television on. Then he backed up to the sofa where their mother already roosted, hands in her lap. Everybody stared as the screen brightened into five animated panels and the orchestrated theme of their favorite show began. When the panels came to life, a cartoon cowboy in the center lit a cigarette, tossed the match away, and wheeled just in time to karate-chop an armed bandit backing out of a saloon. Quickly he then dealt with trouble in two other panels—a gambler trying to cheat at cards, a gunman raising his pistol—and finally he disarmed, with a kiss, a beautiful, knife-wielding lady in a big hoop skirt. As she slumped against the panel wall, the knife rattling from her slack fingers, the cowboy sauntered off into the distance, lighting another smoke while the opening credits rolled.

Mark waited until after the first commercial break, when the drama resumed with the cowboy hero seemingly doomed by the actions of a demented, evil dwarf. When the tension reached its peak, he crawled noiselessly past the end of the couch into the hallway. There he stood up and listened. They'd probably just think he was going to the bathroom anyway, but there was no sense in being careless.

Mark gave a dismissive salute and sauntered dangerously through the kitchen to the shed and outside into the evening. It was warm and moonless, with dozens of stars clustered against the black sky. He changed to an Indian-scout gait—toes pointed in—and stole between the tall elms that flanked the driveway. It seemed to him he was moving silently, but Mr. Man detected him nonetheless, and let out a series of short, sharp barks. Then the rest of the collies began barking and howling.

Mark ran across the Baxter River Road to the dirt road that led down to the woods and through to the river. The dogs howled louder and he sped toward his grandparents' house. His plan was to circle the house to the crab-apple grove, to hide there and lob crab apples onto the flat roof of his aunt Carolyn's at the bottom of the hill. This was to pay back his cousin Arnold Stimpson, who at noon recess that day had belted him in the stomach so hard that Mark had collapsed onto the ground, gasping. Arnold had hulked off without a word, but Mark had known exactly what it was for: Arnold had called a meeting of the Wolf Club on the way to school, and Mark, vice president of the club, had spent recess with Daryl Sleeper instead of attending.

Mark hadn't tattled afterwards, like a little kid would have.

He was going to pay Arnold back on his own.

Mark stole past his grandparents' screened porch, dogtrotted around the garage and past the rain barrel that held his grandfather's outboard. He brushed through their clothesline, tangled momentarily in a pair of damp overalls, and ran into the grove. The living-room window in his aunt's little house flickered with pale light. Mark knew they'd be watching the cowboy show, too. He imagined his cousin running outside, stomping around in the dark without finding Mark, going back in to have the show mostly over. It made him smirk triumphantly to himself.

Mark prowled around the grove until he found a site with a clear shot toward the house and a nearby lilac bush for cover. Then he picked up a couple of small, misshapen crab apples and made sure his throwing motion would clear the branches. He drew back his right arm, imagined the lumpy little apple arcing toward Arnold's roof. He felt his muscles tighten.

But then he couldn't do it.

Arnold would come running outside all right, but he'd either catch Mark tonight or settle with him tomorrow. He wasn't one to let anything go. And Mark didn't want to be slugged again.

He dropped the apples, ran past the clothesline and out the driveway, growling his disappointment. He turned the opposite way from his house and ran down the dirt road, looking ahead at a stand of dead trees where the road curved left. It was swampy in there, and this had choked the young trees; now they stood stiff and bare against the black sky.

On the right was Mrs. Carey's house, where Daryl Sleeper and his sister, Karin, lived. Mrs. Carey was their grandmother, and they were staying with her until their divorced parents, who lived in Portland, figured out how to share them properly. Mark had known them for several months now, and had come to the conclusion that Portland kids were just different. Daryl, for instance, combed his hair straight back so that it lay in parallel lines. He winked, too, and used such foul language that at first Mark would have to think a quick Hail Mary every few minutes. He was more used to it now, though.

Daryl's sister, a grade behind them, was very pretty with mysterious smudges under her eyes, but she was just as odd. Mark remembered how they'd been playing with Daryl's models one day and she'd opened the door and looked in. She'd never said a word, just let her tongue tap against her braces. Then she'd shut the door and left.

"I think she wanted to come in," Mark said after she'd left.

"No shit, Sherlock." It was one of Daryl's favorite things to say.

"I wouldn't mind," Mark said offhandedly.

"Naw, she's crazy," Daryl said. "C'mon, let's go in the garage."

Daryl had a trumpet and a saxophone and a drum set in Mrs. Carey's garage and could play them all. Like Mark, he'd been taking music lessons after school, which is how they'd become friends. For a week now Daryl had been his best friend—secretly, so Arnold wouldn't find out—although a big part of it was Karin. When she stared at him it made him nervous in a way that he was really starting to like.

❧

Mark jumped over the grassy ditch, crossed the lawn, and tapped on Daryl's yellow-lit window. There was a thump and footsteps and then Daryl eased the shade up. His hair looked freshly combed, the lines slightly wavy, like a plowed field. He held a finger against his lips, went back to his bed. He returned and pushed the window up, freezing when it rasped. While they held still there was another noise, something moving quickly off through the bushes on the other side of the road.

"What's that?" Mark whispered.

"Just a little pussy!" Daryl hissed back. He smothered a laugh, clambered out the window, and pulled it almost all the way shut. Then he showed Mark what he'd brought—a long, silver flashlight and his sneakers—and they ran across the road.

Daryl sat on a stump and pulled his sneakers on. He stood up. "Come on!"

"Where?" Mark said.

"Old Captain Lambert's cabin!"

Daryl took off, with Mark close behind. They sprinted around the curve past the swamp and the dead trees and turned onto an old logging road. The road was grown up, and they had to push scratchy brush aside to enter. Daryl turned the flashlight on and they followed its column of light through the woods, up a long hill to the old, abandoned cabin, which sat near the edge of a bluff overlooking the Baxter River. They walked over to the bluff and looked down at the lazy water. Then they went back to the cabin.

Mark had been up here several times before.

Once, he and Arnold had collected dead wood and started a fire in the crumbly old stone fireplace. But the chimney was blocked;

flames had licked out and the cabin had filled with smoke. They'd burst out, through the front door and had run off through the woods, stopping by their grandparents' to look back, certain the place would burn to the ground. Which it probably would have, if Roger Lambert hadn't seen the smoke from the airstrip and come hitching across the old wood road with a fire extinguisher.

When they'd snuck back a week later there were scorch marks on the wooden mantel and blackened rocks around the fireplace, but the cabin was still standing. That was the last time he'd been back, because they'd heard that Mr. Lambert was trying to find out who'd nearly destroyed his great-grandfather's cabin, and Mr. Lambert was a little scary sometimes.

Daryl's flashlight played over the boarded-up front door and windows. They walked around to the other side of the cabin and Daryl knelt by a cellar window and worked the loose frame out of the foundation with his jackknife.

"Ha!" he said, turning and squirming through feetfirst, dropping out of sight.

Mark followed, clawing cobwebs away from his face.

They crossed the damp cellar and went up the stairs. The cellar door was latched, but Daryl used the knife to flip the hook that held it shut.

The boys spent the next half hour kicking around the old cabin, smoking cigarettes from the pack of Luckies Daryl had swiped from his grandmother's stash under the kitchen sink. There wasn't much to see: two rooms, an old set of bedsprings in one; shards of glass on the floor under the window openings; an old print of Quebec City tacked onto the wall, a faded and torn calendar from 1929. Mark took the calendar down and brought it to where Daryl sat on the springs. He wanted to see what day his birthday had been on in

1929, but March was gone from the pages, and he sent the calendar flapping across the room.

Daryl bounced off the springs. "Man, I have to piss." He ran into the other room and after a moment Mark heard him say, "Found the jungle!" and then, "Found the reptile!" He sounded proud, and sometimes Mark felt the same way about himself, not that he'd ever talk out loud about it. He listened to Daryl pissing into the fireplace.

Finally Daryl came back, took the cigarette pack out of his shirt pocket, and knocked a Lucky partway into his palm. "Want another smoke?"

Mark looked at his hand. "No, thanks."

Daryl stuck the pack back in his pocket. He sat down and made the springs creak. "I know a secret."

"Oh yeah?" Mark said.

"Don't know if I should tell you."

Mark felt like Mr. Man, ears pricked. He wasn't going to ask, though. Heroes waited, and after a while they always seemed to find out what they needed to.

"All right," Daryl said. "Somebody likes you."

"Who?"

"Karin. She'll come out if we go back."

Mark's face felt suddenly hot.

"So do you want to?"

"If you do," Mark said, as if his heart wasn't pounding.

The window rasped like before, and again they held still and listened. Then Daryl hooked a leg over the sill, ducked under the sash, and lowered himself in. Mark followed and started to shut the window, but Daryl said, "Leave it up!"

"Okay," Mark said.

"Wait here," Daryl said.

While Daryl was gone Mark looked at the fighter models and another of the Apollo rocket on Daryl's dresser. He was never any good at models because he just wanted to get them done.

You could tell Daryl took his time. There was no extra glue around the seams, no missing pieces. Mark ran his hand over the rocket, then went over to the bed and sat down. A couple of minutes later the door opened and Daryl and Karin tiptoed into the room. Daryl was giggling with his hand over his mouth.

"Shhh!" Karin whispered. Then she said, "Hi."

"Hi," Mark said.

Karin sat on the bed and looked at her brother.

"Go ahead!" Daryl whispered.

"No, you go out, Daryl!"

"All right." Daryl opened the door and left.

Karin gave Mark a flicker of a smile. Her eyes were like black marbles and her short hair was very dark and thick. Mark tried to smile back, but he was short of breath, like he'd been swimming underwater, and it made the smile feel crooked on his face.

"Want to do something?" Karin said then.

"Like what?"

"Want to kiss?" Karin whispered.

"Sure." Mark barely got the word out. He sort of pushed his face toward Karin, but just as his lips touched hers Daryl opened the door and stuck his head into the room.

"Not now!" Karin whispered.

Daryl shut the door again.

Karin leaned her whole body against Mark. She put her hand on his side and pressed her lips right up against his. He could feel the braces under her lip. She flicked her tongue against his teeth.

"Huh!" The sound flew out of Mark's mouth, and Karin jerked away, looking at him wide-eyed.

Mark couldn't talk. Everything had gone thick and smoky inside him. He put his hands on her arms and put his lips back on hers. Their tongues touched and then, as if on its own, his hand slid over her stomach to her small breast. She made a sound and her breath came warm against his face. When she put her hand on his knee he cried, "Oh!"

Karin jumped up, her eyes wide and shiny. She backed to the door and reached behind her for the knob. She opened the door and ran down the hall, her feet thumping softly.

Daryl came in and shut the door. "What'd she do?"

"Nothing."

"I saw you two!"

Mark didn't say anything to that. He didn't want to talk to Daryl just now. He wanted to be alone so he could think about what had just happened.

"Do you like her?" Daryl said.

"Sure," Mark said. "I'd better get home."

He went to the window, put his head and arms through, and toppled out, somersaulting and rolling to his feet. His ears were ringing like crazy.

Daryl stuck his head out. "See you tomorrow."

"Okay!" Mark whispered back.

Daryl shut the window and Mark ran across the lawn and set off down the road. It was very dark and the sky seemed bigger, with more and brighter stars. Thousands, he thought, maybe millions.

After a while he went back to his hero walk. When he got to his grandparents', he remembered about Arnold, and without hesitating he ran back to the crab-apple orchard. He picked up a pair of big, smooth apples and held them in his hands, looking down the hill. Before he could chicken out again he whipped one through the dark and a second later heard it thump on Aunt Carolyn's roof.

It was louder than he'd expected, and it bounced almost all the way to the old chicken coop behind the house. But he still threw the other one. There was a second loud bang, and he hid behind the lilac and waited.

After a few seconds Arnold came outside. He just stood there with his hands on his hips until the peepers raised their voices off in the woods. They'd shut up, but now they got louder and louder until his cousin went back in and slammed the door and then they stopped again.

Mark took his sweet time ambling home.

It was ten o'clock and he lay in bed listening to the dogs. His father must have gone outside again. He'd been on his way through the shed when Mark had gotten home. He'd had his pipe in his hand and had stared at Mark walking past him to the kitchen.

"Hold on there, boy," he'd said.

Mark had stopped by the kitchen door. He could hear the TV in the living room. He'd already missed a couple of good shows, not that he really cared.

"Just where have you been?" his father said.

"Outside," Mark said.

"Where outside?"

"Just outside."

"Are you being smart?"

"No!"

The dogs yipped and yowled, their voices rising, then trailing off. Mark and his father turned their heads to listen. When the noise stopped, Mark looked back at his father.

"Maybe you should go right to your room," his father said.

"Why?"

"Because I said to."

"That's not fair."

"Fair's got nothing to do with it."

"No shit, Sherlock," Mark said. A thrill ran through him.

Mark's father grabbed him under one arm and yanked him onto his toes. Mark flinched but didn't cower, and they stared fiercely at one another until his father's face softened, as if he'd just remembered who Mark was. He let Mark down. "Ah hell, I'm sorry, old kid."

"No you're not," Mark said coldly. He saw the hurt in his father's eyes, but turned away just the same and marched up the stairs. He reached the top and looked down. His father was standing still with his hands in his pockets, and Mark felt another stab of regret. But he kept right on going.

It was good to be under the cool sheets in the dark. Below, the TV was playing, and he could tell which show it was, but he still didn't care that much. He didn't care about hurting his father's feelings, either. There were more important things to think about.

He imagined Karin Sleeper's dark eyes and how her body had felt in his hands. It was amazing just how solid and *real* girls were when you actually felt them. It was like touching a deer or something. He got a little short of breath, and reached to open his window wider. It stuck, and when he pushed harder it banged against its stop.

One of the dogs woofed in the pen. Then another one yipped. Then Mr. Man joined in and quickly they were all in full cry. Mark put his arms on the sill and listened. They sounded different tonight.

He'd never heard them sound like this.

The dogs kept at it as if they'd never stop. After a while they didn't even sound like collies. They could just as easily have been wild animals, out in the woods. Coyotes on the hunt, maybe, or a pack of wolves, loping through the dark, chasing something irresistible.

Ted

The summer Ted Soule turned eight, a family of Russians came to Baxter, moving into the farmhouse on the other side of the big hayfield. They kept to themselves, and all Ted knew about them after a month was that someone over there played the piano. When the wind was right he could just hear it from his window, delicate as a memory.

Lying in bed, listening, he would imagine them gathered around as their father played. There were supposed to be two kids, according to his mother, and Ted wondered if they would become his friends.

There was something wrong with him that made it hard to make friends. He was generally ignored at school, unless somebody like Arnold Stimpson decided to push him around, but maybe these kids, being from another country, would see him differently.

One morning early in August he finally saw them. They were in the hayfield: a girl and a smaller boy, running and stooping. He dug his binoculars out from under his mattress but still couldn't tell what they were up to; finally, he pulled on his clothes and ran downstairs and out to the field.

He halted a respectful distance away, looking down at his sneakers when the Russian girl glanced over. The blueberry plants were dry and dusty, and he heard them crackling as the girl walked up, and then he saw her saddle shoes.

"Look at me," the girl said. "What's your name?"

"Ted," he managed to say, but he still couldn't look.

"My name is Nadia Myachin," she said proudly, "and that's my stupid brother, Gregor."

"Shut up, Nadia." The boy was on his hands and knees, staring.

"Why won't you look at me?" Nadia said.

Ted finally glanced up. She was beautiful, with high cheekbones, bright blue eyes, and golden hair that fell over her shoulders. The silence grew between them until finally he said, "I live right over there."

"Yes, of course," Nadia said.

"What are you guys doing?"

Gregor was patting the bushes with one hand, then the other.

"Looking for grasshoppers," Nadia said.

She explained that the grasshoppers were for their pet bird, Yuri. They had found him with an injured wing and their father had let them keep him, but they'd had to promise he would have plenty to eat.

Ted was impressed about the bird, but disappointed with the way they talked; he'd imagined them sounding like Illya Kuryakin on *The Man from U.N.C.L.E.* But he was happy when Nadia asked if he wanted to help, and for the next few minutes he stuck close to her side, moving through the blueberry bushes, grabbing the squirmy grasshoppers, carefully lifting the punctured lid on a coffee can and dropping them in.

And he was thrilled to be asked to their house to help feed Yuri. It didn't even bother him that Nadia won the race back. It upset Gregor, though; he ran stubbornly and cried when he couldn't catch up.

Mr. Myachin welcomed Ted with a satisfyingly thick accent. He was big and red-faced. His wife was slender and quiet. Yuri, it turned out, lived in a jungle of potted plants on top of their grand piano. He liked the music, Nadia said.

She put a grasshopper down and Yuri hopped out and gulped it. Nadia wouldn't let anyone else feed him. You had to aim the grasshoppers just right, she said, or they'd jump off the piano and run all over the house. Gregor growled at this, but still handed Nadia the grasshoppers one at a time. When there were only a few left, he let Ted hold the coffee can, so he could reach in and select a grasshopper.

Yuri ate all the grasshoppers and then hopped back behind the plants.

Ted followed Nadia and Gregor into the kitchen, where Mr. Myachin smiled at them and said, "Show hands!"

Ted watched Nadia and Gregor open their hands, and then did so himself. There were brown stains on all their palms.

"Tobacco juice!" Mr. Myachin boomed.

"I call it grasshopper poop," Nadia whispered to Ted.

"No swearing!" Gregor hissed.

"That's not swearing!" Nadia hissed back.

"You, boy," Mr. Myachin said. "Can swim?"

"A little," Ted said.

"Good! Come and swim, wash away tobacco juice!"

Nadia and Gregor cheered and said, "Come on!" to Ted. They ran upstairs and Nadia darted into her bedroom and shut the door. Gregor took Ted into his bedroom and gave him a red bathing suit from his dresser. He took out a blue one for himself, with a cartoon Road Runner emblazoned on the leg. Ted was impressed with the room's neatness. There was a world globe on Gregor's dresser and a map of Soviet Russia on his wall.

They met Nadia back in the hallway and ran downstairs.

"Where are we going?" Ted said.

"The quarry!" Nadia and Gregor shouted.

Ted wasn't supposed to go to the quarry, but he figured it would be all right with Mr. Myachin along.

He trailed them out of the house. Mr. Myachin walked with his shoulders back, swinging his arms. He led the way down the field to the bushes and through to a pine-and-birch wood and through the wood to the quarry. Mr. Myachin talked the whole way about what a great country America was, how lucky they were to live where you could have a big house and make a good living and go for a swim anytime you wanted, and nobody ever stopped you to ask what you were up to.

It made Ted happy and proud, as if he'd had something to do with it.

The path led to a rocky stretch of ground that ended in an outcropping over the flooded quarry. Carefully they descended a steep trail to a flat ledge by the water. Mr. Myachin set the towels down, took off his shirt—his belly was big and white compared to his tanned arms—and dove in with a thunderclap of a splash. He swam out into the middle, blowing a stream of water high into the air like a whale. The children laughed and jumped in carefully, chins high to keep their faces dry. The boys dog-paddled, staying close to the ledge, but Nadia swam right out in a proud, stiff-necked crawl.

After a while Mr. Myachin caught hold of a rope that hung down from the cables that crisscrossed the top of the quarry. The rope was thick and had a thinner line attached that dragged in the water. Holding the thin rope in his teeth, Mr. Myachin swam back to the ledge, then climbed up to the outcropping and, after waving, ran off the edge of the rock, the rope in his hands. The rope jerked him into an arc out over the water, where he let go and hung suspended, twisting slowly, before falling the rest of the way into the drink with another thunderous splash.

Nadia, Gregor, and Ted cheered.

"My turn!" Nadia said when Mr. Myachin pulled himself out.

"No, not for little kids," Mr. Myachin said.

"I'm *not* a little kid!" Nadia said.

"You are little kid one more year!" Mr. Myachin was vigorously toweling himself off.

Nadia sat down on the ledge with her chin in her hands. She stayed put when Ted and Gregor jumped in for a last swim.

When Ted got home he told his mother about the bird and the grasshoppers and the quarry, and she said, "As long as there's a grown-up along."

"Okay," Ted said.

"Were they nice people?"

"Yes," Ted said. "They liked me, too."

Ted went to visit several times over the next few weeks. Once he even stayed overnight, sleeping on a cot in Gregor's room, listening to Mr. Myachin play lively music on the piano.

Ted still felt pretty lucky they'd moved to Baxter. Gregor was kind of a pill, and Nadia was five years older, but it still seemed like they were getting to be friends. He pictured them getting off the bus together and walking into school. It was nice, too, to feed Yuri and to go swimming anytime you wanted. Mr. Myachin was always willing, and Mrs. Myachin would walk down and sit on the rocks if her husband was away.

One day late in August, though—a day so hot that the tar road had gone soft—both Mr. and Mrs. Myachin decided to go into town to shop for a new car. They were going to Cousins Motors, they said, and the number would be by the phone just in case, and there was to be no swimming until they got back.

"Be good!" Mr. Myachin said as they were leaving.

It was a Saturday, and after feeding Yuri the children settled onto the couch in the living room to watch cartoons. Ted didn't mind—it was just a delay—and Gregor loved cartoons almost as much as swimming anyway.

But Nadia complained and fidgeted. Every time she moved, her skin made a sound like Scotch tape against the leather couch, and finally she said, "Unnhhh!" and jumped up. She put her hands on her hips and said it was stupid to stay inside and boil when she was perfectly capable of being the grown-up, since she would be an eighth grader in the fall.

"You are not a grown-up!" Gregor yelled, his eyes fixed on the television.

"Shut up," Nadia said. "Grasshopper Greg."

Ted knew that was supposed to mean Gregor had made tobacco juice in his pants.

Nadia put her face down close to her brother's and laughed. Gregor crossed his arms and scowled at the TV, where Wile E. Coyote had just run off a cliff. When he hit there was a puff of smoke and the Road Runner beeped happily and zoomed off.

"All right, then, I'll call and ask permission!" Nadia said.

She marched into the kitchen and Ted heard her dial the rotary phone. Then he heard her say, "Oh, thank you, Father!" in a very loud voice. She hung up the phone so that it dinged and came back into the living room.

Mr. Myachin had told her it was all right this once, but they had to promise to mind Nadia and do everything she said. She switched off the TV, and Gregor put on his blue Road Runner bathing suit and loaned Ted the red one again. Nadia met them downstairs with three towels slung over her shoulder.

They walked past the piano, where Yuri cocked his head from between the plants.

"Can we bring grasshoppers back?" Ted said.

"Bring the coffee can," Nadia said.

Ted grabbed the can off the top of the piano and they ran out of the house and followed Nadia as she skipped across the shaggy lawn to the path. Nadia could skip very fast, almost as if her feet didn't touch the ground, and the boys had to run hard to try and keep up. When Ted stopped to catch his breath, Gregor kept running slowly, with his fists clenched. In the field Nadia slowed to a walk. When the boys caught up there were dozens of grasshoppers jumping around.

They went single file along a path that led downhill to the quarry. The air cooled as they came to the outcropping overlooking the water.

Ted felt funny to be here alone, but Nadia dropped the towels and raised her arms in the air and said, "Ahhh!" Then she walked out on the outcropping and put a hand on the heavy, cabled rope that Mr. Myachin had left tied to a bush.

"I might just take a swing," she announced.

"Father said no!" Gregor said.

Nadia stuck out her tongue.

Gregor picked up a rock and threw it as hard as he could against the wall of the quarry. Then he turned and started carefully down the rocky trail to the flat ledge. Ted followed, picking his way between the rock edges. When he reached the bottom he saw Nadia was still on the outcropping, holding the rope in one hand, leaning back against its weight.

"I'll tell!" Gregor yelled.

"Go ahead, Grasshopper Greg!"

Nadia stuck her bottom out and snapped the edge of her bathing suit against her hip. She ran to the edge and skidded to a stop, teetering, and grinned down at Gregor. But Gregor only crossed his arms and glared, so she backed away again, and this time ran right off the rock, jumping way out and falling, pulling the slack out of the rope.

Ted waited for her to swing out over the water, but when she reached the rope's limit it snapped itself right out of her hands, sending her into a long tumble that ended in an awkward, flat splash into the water.

The boys ran to the edge of the ledge, and when Nadia reappeared, her long hair fanning out, Ted clapped his hands and even

Gregor yelled, *Wheee!* But Nadia only looked at them and sank again. Bubbles broke the surface and a shock went through Ted. He held his breath, but she didn't come back. Finally Gregor said, "Come on!" and they waded out until the rock dropped away and then dog-paddled toward the rope trembling into the water.

They couldn't find Nadia. Ted even put his face into the water and opened his eyes. Finally they were exhausted and had to splash back to the ledge. They climbed to the top of the quarry and ran gasping back to the field and staggered through the springing grasshoppers to the house.

When they burst into the kitchen, Mrs. Myachin smiled. "Did you see my new car, you boys?"

But Mr. Myachin frowned at their wet suits. "Where is Nadia?"

Gregor sobbed.

Mr. Myachin looked fiercely at Ted, and when Ted's mouth trembled he yanked the door open and tore out of the house. The boys and Mrs. Myachin ran after him. Ted had never seen anyone's mother run like that before. When they got to the field, Mr. Myachin was gone, but the grasshoppers were all stirred up.

The boys followed Mrs. Myachin across the field and into the woods. They kept up with her, even though Ted's legs were heavy as granite and Gregor was gasping and straining.

"Oh, please God, no," Mrs. Myachin kept saying.

Mr. Myachin was standing in the quarry entrance with Nadia in his arms, both of them dripping water onto the rock.

"Run back!" he said, looking at his daughter's slack face. "Call ambulance!" Mrs. Myachin ran off, knock-kneed, choking.

Mr. Myachin put Nadia down and knelt over her. He blew into her mouth, pushed on her thin chest. Her hair was in the dirt, and when Gregor tried to brush it clean, Mr. Myachin shoved him away with one hand.

Gregor fell backwards and started crying again.

"Shut up," Mr. Myachin said. He blew again into Nadia's mouth, pushed rhythmically on her chest. Water came out of her mouth. He kept at it until a siren wailed in the distance, and then he picked her up and ran heavily back through the woods.

Ted and Gregor fell far behind, stumbling through the field and up to the house.

There was an ambulance in the driveway, bouncing red flashes off the Myachins' new car. Mrs. Myachin was looking into the ambulance with her hands clenched at her sides, and when the boys came up she turned and said, "Gregor, you go to Teddy's house and wait there."

Men were talking urgently inside the ambulance. Mrs. Myachin took an awkward step up then, and a man with a big, pale mustache glanced in a stricken way at the two boys as he helped her inside. The man pulled the door shut and the ambulance zoomed off, flashing and beeping.

Ted and Gregor looked at each other and started across the hayfield. It seemed to take forever, grasshoppers springing up on both sides. Neither boy said anything the whole way.

Toward the end of that summer the Myachins sold their house so they could move back to Russia. Ted's mother said it was because they needed someone to talk to in their own language.

"It's so sad, Teddy," she said.

Ted hadn't been to visit since that hot Saturday, but when he heard they were leaving, he'd asked if it would be all right to go and say good-bye to Gregor, and his mother said she thought it would, but he should hurry because it was almost suppertime.

So Ted set out across the hayfield and knocked on the side door, the one with the metal latch that the Myachins used instead of their front door.

After a few seconds Gregor opened the door and looked out at Ted.

"Hi," Ted said.

"Hi," Gregor said. "You can come in if you want."

The living room was nearly empty of furniture, but the grand piano was still there and Yuri was, too. He hopped out from behind a plant and looked at them.

"Are you really going back to Russia?" Ted said.

"Yes," Gregor said. He put his finger on a piano key and played a high, plinky note. Then he put his hands in his pockets.

Yuri looked at them with his head cocked.

"Want to go get some grasshoppers?" Ted asked.

"Okay," Gregor said.

The boys went out though the side door. The field was cropped now and it was cooler, but there were still a few grasshoppers dodging around at half speed. They hadn't brought a container—the coffee can was still down at the quarry, Ted remembered—but they managed to grab enough with both hands to make Yuri a reasonable meal. Ted could feel them squirming inside his fists. He walked back with his hands out to the side.

In the house he and Gregor put them on the piano one at a time and Yuri chased them down and ate them. But Gregor aimed the last one wrong and it jumped off and hopped down the short hallway to the kitchen.

"Catch him!" Gregor said.

Ted ran after the grasshopper, dropping to his knees and trapping it against the baseboard next to the kitchen table, where Gregor's parents stood wrapping dishes in newspaper. He squeezed the grasshopper and looked up at them.

Mr. Myachin just stared back with his big, dark eyes, but Mrs. Myachin patted him on the head. Ted pulled the grasshopper's legs off so it couldn't escape again. He was very angry at it for trying to get away. He took it back to the piano and gave it to Yuri, who pecked it twice and swallowed it down. Ted gave him the legs, and Yuri ate those too, then cocked his head and ruffled his wings. Ted thought he looked pretty healthy. He asked Gregor if they were going to turn him loose when they moved back to Russia. Gregor said they already had, a couple of times, but Yuri kept coming back and tapping on the window.

"Really?" Ted said.

"Yes," Gregor said.

Mrs. Myachin came into the room, looking tired.

"I'm sorry, Teddy," she said, "but you have to go home. Gregor must get to work and pack." She patted his head again and went back to the kitchen.

Gregor led Ted to the side door and held out his hand. Ted noticed a smear of tobacco juice on his palm. They put their hands together and solemnly shook.

"I'll probably never see you again," Gregor said. He jiggled the latch and opened it and they went into the yard. "My father said he'll leave a window open for Yuri when we leave," Gregor said.

"Good," Ted said. His whole chest felt tight.

"Maybe he'll fly over to your house."

"We don't have a piano," Ted said, and then he turned and walked away. He couldn't look back, not even when Gregor called, "Bye!"

When he heard the door shut, it freed him to run. He sprinted across the hayfield, trying to stomp on the grasshoppers. At home he dodged past his mother and ran to his bedroom. When she tapped on his door he said, "Stay out!" because he couldn't talk to anyone just then.

In bed he rolled onto his stomach. The sheet went wet against his face and the breeze through his window made the sheet cool. He got the hiccups and held his pillow over his head until they went away. Then he threw the pillow on the floor and turned onto his back. He held his breath, and it got so quiet that he could feel his heart beating.

Then he heard the piano faintly from the Russians' house. It was a sad song that made Ted's breath come in hitches. After a while it changed and became like the music to a cartoon, louder and jangly. Then it stopped altogether. Ted lay still, waiting, but the music hadn't resumed by the time his mother called him to supper.

That was the last time Ted heard the piano.

Some other people moved into the farmhouse that fall, and he never saw the Myachins again. But he never forgot them, either. He remembered them whenever he looked at the farmhouse, or thought about the quarry. He remembered when school began and he still didn't have any friends, and again when summer returned and he walked through the field and grasshoppers jumped out of his way.

Oh, he never forgot them, not ever. Even thirty and forty years later, after everything else that had happened in his life, Ted Soule would sometimes come slowly awake early in the morning and realize that he was holding his breath and listening, as if there might be music outside, or maybe even a beautiful girl saying, "Look at me."

Arnold

Arnold Stimpson walked up the newly plowed road, feeling the brittle cold on his face. He knew that a week was probably not long enough to have stayed away, but his aunt was just going to have to live with it. He was tired of waiting by himself.

He clumped in his rubber boots up to the River Road and crossed to where his cousins were waiting. He dropped his paper bag beside their array of lunch boxes and looked at Julie, the nicest cousin, in her puffy yellow jacket. He could hear their dogs barking from behind the house. It always bothered him that their dogs had to stay in a pen.

"Hi, Arnold," Julie said.

"Hi," Arnold said.

Linda, the oldest cousin, stood atop the snowbank. She had a puffy winter jacket, too, a red one. All the cousins had them.

Arnold was still wearing his fall jacket, which was too short in the arms and more like a heavy flannel shirt, anyway.

"I thought you weren't allowed up here anymore," Linda said.

"It's a free country."

"It's private property."

"Not the road."

Arnold's cousin Mark stood beside Linda. Arnold couldn't tell if he was still mad. He knew his aunt Lois was from the way she was staring out the kitchen window. He looked back at her until she turned and spoke to someone he couldn't see.

A few seconds later Uncle Mike came outside and got in the car. He backed out of the driveway, drove up to the crossing, leaned across the seat, and rolled down the passenger window. Uncle Mike had reddish-brown hair and a snub nose, like Arnold's mother. Like Arnold, too, for that matter. Arnold thought he looked more like a Mitchell than the cousins did.

"I'm surprised to see you here," Uncle Mike said.

Arnold looked at his boots.

"I thought we'd decided you would wait at your own house."

"I did, for a week," Arnold said.

Uncle Mike frowned. Then he looked up at Mark and raised his eyebrows.

"I don't care." Mark touched under his eye.

Arnold wished now that he hadn't socked him. But Mark shouldn't have said he was stupid, either.

"Can you keep your hands to yourself?" Uncle Mike said.

"I will," Arnold said.

"All right, we'll give it one more try."

Uncle Mike slid back behind the wheel and let the car idle toward the road. When it was even with the big snowbank he waved over the roof.

"Bye, Daddy!" the cousins all cried.

The Plymouth turned onto the tar road, and the cousins walked out to watch, the arms of their jackets whispering against their sides. Then Julie yelled, "Bus coming!" and they hustled back, grabbing their lunch boxes and lining up according to age.

The bus came hissing to a stop and Mrs. Morrison levered open the door. Arnold waited until last, then climbed the steps and followed Mark down the aisle toward the Hurd brothers, who lived on the Desert Road and always got on first.

Mark said, "Hey," and slid into the seat opposite the Hurds. He didn't shove over, so Arnold took the next seat. The bus low-geared into a turn onto the dirt road and started off.

Arnold sat eyeing the Hurds. He called them the Turds, but Mark didn't think that was funny anymore. He liked them now, and had even gone over to play on the desert a couple of times. Arnold still thought they were sissies, though, especially Larry, the older one, who had wispy blond hair and wore gloves instead of mittens and was always reading books. He had his nose in a book right now. His head nodded as the bus bumped down the dirt road, but he kept right on reading, snapping a page over. He read very fast, which was another thing Arnold didn't like.

"Whatcha reading, Larry Turd?" Arnold said.

Larry patiently swiveled the cover toward Arnold: *The Wind in the Willows*.

"That's a girl's book!" Arnold jeered. He looked at Mark, but Mark just moved impatiently on the bus seat. Arnold sat back and crossed his arms. Then he reached out and poked Larry Hurd in the arm.

"Larry Turd, the Girl in the Willows!" he chanted, but Larry ignored him. When Arnold, after waiting a minute or two, knocked the book out of his hands, Larry's brother picked it up off the floor and said, "Why don't you lay off?"

Lucas Hurd was younger than Larry, but bigger. They didn't look much alike, but that was because they were stepbrothers. Mark had told Arnold that after he'd come back from playing with them. Neither of them knew exactly what a stepbrother was, though.

"Why don't you make me?" Arnold said to Lucas.

"Somebody's going to someday." Lucas handed his brother the book.

Larry brushed it off and started right in reading again.

"Too bad *you're* too chicken," Arnold said.

"Fighting's stupid."

"That's what all the chickens say."

Lucas faced forward and didn't reply.

They rode along in silence until the little set-back house where Arnold lived with his mother came into view. Lucas Hurd glanced at Arnold then and whispered something to his brother, who took one hand from his book and smothered a laugh.

"What's so funny?" Arnold said.

"Nothing." Lucas was still grinning.

"Cut it out, Luke," Mark warned from across the aisle.

Arnold looked at Mark, then back at Lucas.

"What?" Lucas said. "I was just gonna say that we might be chickens . . ."

"Shut *up*, Luke!"

". . . but at least we don't live in a chicken coop!"

Lucas grinned at his own audacity, but only until Arnold stood up. Everybody got quiet then while Arnold swayed in the aisle with his hands on the seats. Then he leaned over and started punching. Larry Hurd ducked down to the floor while Lucas tried to swing back. Arnold struck raised arms and the hard back of the seat, and finally—with a meaty smack—Lucas Hurd's cheek.

Lucas let out a squeal for Mrs. Morrison, but she was already pulling the bus over to the side of the road. When she hit the brakes, Arnold stumbled to his knees. As soon as he got up she had him by the ear. She pulled him down the aisle and said, "Sit!" when they got to the stairwell.

Arnold sat in the slushy dirt from everybody's boots.

Mrs. Morrison glared around until the bus grew quiet, then got back behind the wheel.

Soon they were rambling along the dirt road again, stopping to pick up Daryl and Karin Sleeper and the Philips kids. They all squeezed past Arnold and moved down the aisle. Daryl sat with Mark Mitchell, and Karin sat with Emily Philips. She turned to look at Mark and Daryl whispering as the bus started off. Then she faced front again.

Outside, fat snowflakes began to fall.

The bus reached the turnaround at the end of the road where you could see the river. Then it headed back. When it got to Arnold's house all the kids looked out the window. Arnold looked too, through the tall, smudged glass panels in the door.

You couldn't really tell that it had been a chicken coop, he thought. Not unless somebody told you—somebody like Mark. Mark knew, because his father had helped their grandfather work on it, finishing what Arnold's stupid father had left undone. They'd added glass windows and shingles and a door. It had been a brooder coop anyway, not a real coop, like the empty two-story building that still stood behind it. Arnold could just remember when the big coop was full of chickens. He remembered his grandfather chopping their heads off, and how they ran around afterwards and everybody jumped so as not to get splashed.

The bus moved down the road and some of the kids turned their heads, as if Arnold's house were a roadside attraction, like the Hurd family's made-up desert. Then they were swinging onto the tar road, and everyone faced forward as they rolled on to the school.

❧

During recess, when Arnold heard Daryl Sleeper say *chicken coop*, he clamped a headlock on him and rubbed his face in the snow. One of the teachers ran over to stop it, and then told Arnold to follow him inside.

Arnold had to spend the rest of the afternoon in the principal's office, at a table in the corner. He didn't mind that so much. It was better than being in class, with everybody whispering. But then Mrs. Kimball sat down with him and started in about his family. Mrs. Kimball wasn't all that old but had gray hair. She wore it in a ponytail that sat on her shoulder like a pet squirrel.

"It's never easy growing up without a dad," she said to Arnold. "But you still have to behave yourself. Otherwise you'll spend your whole life in and out of trouble. You don't want that, do you, Arnold?"

"Nuh-uh," Arnold said.

Mrs. Kimball let the ponytail slip through her fingers while she talked.

Arnold pretended to pay attention, but he couldn't really, or it made him feel awful. He hated talking about his father. He mumbled every now and then so she'd *think* he was listening. Meanwhile, he thought about other stuff.

He thought about his uncle and cousins and their big house up on the corner. He thought about the Red Sox. Then he thought some more about the big coop—how it made echoes when you walked around inside.

The big coop was pretty spooky. There were round metal bins where the chickens used to eat, and all these weird little "spectacles" lying around that they'd worn on their beaks. They weren't really spectacles; you couldn't see through them. They were something the chickens wore so they wouldn't turn into killers. His grandfather had told him that without the spectacles they would pick one poor chicken out and gang up on it. They'd all chase it into a corner and peck at it until it died. For some reason the spectacles stopped that from happening, but Arnold had never figured out exactly why.

"Are you listening to me, Arnold?" Mrs. Kimball said.

"Uh-huh."

Arnold had to apologize to Daryl Sleeper and the Hurds and Mrs. Morrison before he was allowed back on the bus. The Hurd brothers were being picked up by their father, and when Arnold walked over to say he was sorry, Mr. Hurd made them all shake hands. Then he said to Larry, "Next time, punch him back, right in the nose," and Larry looked at the ground.

Arnold sat behind Mark on the bus and told him he could come over and have some coffee cake if he wanted. His mother had brought it home from the shoe shop two days before. Mark, who never got coffee cake at home (Aunt Lois didn't think it was good for you), was a little friendlier after that, and said he would try to sneak out.

He had to sneak because Aunt Lois wouldn't let him play at Arnold's anymore after Arnold had let Mark shoot the .22 his dad had left behind. They'd taken it into the woods behind the big coop and had shot at a pine tree. Arnold's grandfather had heard the shots and come down into the woods and taken the rifle away. He'd told Mark's parents, and Uncle Mike had lectured them about guns. Afterward Arnold's mother had hidden the rifle, although it didn't take him long to find it in a closet behind her coats, the same place she hid everything.

Mark finally came outside and ran past the elms and down the driveway and across River Road. The dogs were barking and he sprinted right past Arnold with a laugh, and Arnold had to hustle to catch up. Then Mark slowed down and they walked together along the dirt road.

It was getting dark already, but Arnold could see a car in their driveway. He ran up and looked it over—an old Nash Rambler; he knew his cars—without letting himself think that his father had decided to come home. He wasn't *that* stupid. There were little boxes and snap-shut cases on the backseat, along with a fishing rod and tackle box. His father had hated fishing.

"Whose car is that?" Mark said.

"Somebody that gave her a ride home, I guess."

They walked downhill toward Arnold's house and the big two-story coop.

Arnold opened the screen door and they went inside just as the curtain parted in the doorway across the room and a short man with a red face ducked out. The man saw them and grinned.

"Well, hello there, gentlemen!" he said. "School's out, I take it?" He looked at his silver wristwatch, shoved his shirttail into his pants.

Arnold's mother came out. "You had to lallygag, didn't you, Frank?"

"Whose fault was that?" the man said.

Arnold's mother giggled and raked a hand through her reddish hair. "I guess you caught me, Arnold!" she said. "But you didn't have to bring company! How are you, Marcus?"

"Okay, Aunt Carolyn."

"How's things up at the plantation?"

"Okay." Mark looked at Arnold. "Maybe I'd better go."

Arnold shrugged as if he didn't care.

Mark turned his eyes toward the kitchen table.

"Can Mark take a piece of coffee cake?" Arnold asked.

"Why not?" Arnold's mother said.

Arnold peeled the waxed paper off, cut a piece of the coffee cake, and handed it to Mark.

Mark said, "Thanks!" and took off out the door.

Arnold saw him run past the window, stuffing the coffee cake into his mouth.

"Time for me to be running along, too," the man said.

Arnold left them hugging in the kitchen corner. He walked through the living room and parted the curtain to his bedroom. They didn't have doors to their rooms here in the old brooder coop. He made a face and flopped on his bed with his hands behind his head.

After a minute his mother walked up and pulled the curtain aside.

"I'm going for a ride, honey. You be good; have some coffee cake yourself. I'll be back in a little while."

"Where are you going?" Arnold said.

"Just for a ride. Be good, now!"

Arnold heard the front door shut. He went to the window and watched his mother run up the path with her arms swinging across her body, like a cheerleader. The man named Frank pushed the passenger door open for her from the inside and she got in and slammed it shut. They backed onto the road and rode up toward the crossing.

When they were gone Arnold lay back on the bed, thinking every swear word he knew. Then he got up and went down to his mother's room. He ducked under the curtain and took the .22 out of the closet.

Remembering about it had made him want to shoot it again. He still had some of the little shells under his bed. He put them in his pocket, took the rifle outside to the big coop. She'd never even notice it was gone.

The coop's door hung on one hinge and there was a fan of fine snow on the floorboards. It was cold as anything. He ran up the stairs and hid the rifle and shells behind a feeder near a corner.

Then he went back into the house. He took the rest of the coffee cake over to the couch and turned on the TV.

Arnold was lying down when his mother finally came home. He said, "Hi!," but she didn't answer. She banged into something and then it was quiet.

Arnold left her alone for an hour, but finally got too hungry. It was way past suppertime. He tiptoed up to her curtain and listened to her breathing.

"Mum?" he said.

She went on breathing.

"Mum?" Arnold said again. "Can we have supper?"

"Can't a person take a nap?" his mother said.

"I'm hungry!" Arnold yelled.

His mother made the bed creak and stomped toward the doorway, but got tangled in the curtain. While she was swatting it away Arnold grabbed his jacket and ran outside. He stuffed his hands into the pockets and walked toward the road through an inch of new snow.

He could see his breath, and a cold breeze pecked at his cheeks and the tips of his ears. It made him wish he'd had time to get his cap with the earmuffs. Down the road he could see his grandfather's house all lit up. But his grandfather would just send him home. The cousins' big house was all lit up, too. He could walk up there; he'd done it before when his mother was on the warpath. He even took a couple of steps that way, picturing warm rooms, cousins sprawled on the floor with comic books, his uncle reading the newspaper in his recliner. But his aunt would probably slam the door in his face.

He glanced back at his house and, behind it, the two-story coop.

At least he could get out of the wind.

Arnold trotted down the hill and ducked past the cockeyed door. It was cold and dark inside the coop. He climbed the stairs, feeling his way, retrieved the .22, and loaded one of the shells through its side gate.

He marched around like a soldier for a while, kicking the spectacles out of his way, and when he got tired of that, he knelt by a window and looked through the scope. The streetlight at the crossing jumped into view. A car cleared the woods on the right. It was like watching a TV show.

He followed the car past the cousins' house until it disappeared behind the bushes on the left, then swung the barrel back and stopped when he saw his aunt in the kitchen window. He watched her laugh and wave a wooden spoon and was surprised when the .22 spat. It didn't make very much noise.

He quickly slid another shell in, so it would be like nothing had happened. He looked through the scope again and saw Uncle Mike come outside, sort of crouching and looking around.

When the .22 went off again, Uncle Mike ducked back into the house.

Arnold laid the rifle down then so it wouldn't shoot anymore. He hoped it hadn't hit anyone. He blew on his hands and stuck them in his jacket pockets. It was so cold!

After a while he could hear a siren. It got louder and closer, and he waited to see what would happen. He'd be just as glad if somebody would show up. It was freezing in the coop, and it was getting creepy, too, because he couldn't keep from thinking about those chickens.

He kept imagining a whole gang of them, moving through the building without their spectacles. He could almost hear them, scratching from room to room, getting closer all the time.

Russell

I stop with the ashtrays, take a good look through the window at the big white owl sitting on the wind-sock pole. It's nice, almost like a piece of Alaska has followed me home. I watch him ruffling himself, and I think about Dora O'Malley and Nakasuk.

I space out a little until the kid from the commuter airline says, "Earth to Russ." Then I look over my shoulder. This kid is droopy-eyed, like he never gets enough sleep. Which he probably doesn't, since he recently married a girl with large breasts and sweet, sad eyes.

"Whatcha got out there?" he says.

"Come see." I look back at the owl.

He steps around his counter and scuffs over. The lobby wall is all glass, and I point out at the big white bird. "Don't usually get this far south."

"Huh," the kid says.

"Guess he's having some tough luck."

"He'll have more if somebody lands on him." Then he yawns until his jaw snaps. He's too tired and not bright enough to be all that interested. He graduated from Baxter High, same as me, but I've seen the illiterate notes he leaves around for Roger Lambert, who manages the airport and runs the air taxi, and also just happens to be the guy who talked me into coming back to Maine.

The kid yawns again. *Snap*.

Outside, the owl swoops low over the field and sprints for the trees.

I go back to my janitorial duties, but my head's still in Alaska. I'm thinking birds, and I'm thinking Dora. Birds used to mean nothing to me, right? But she had feeders all over her yard, and bird books in her Klondike trailer. She was a good gal, and it was fun learning from her. There's a lot to birds, it turns out. Owls, especially.

I move around the lobby, emptying the tops of the ashtrays into their hollow bases.

It's a pain to be back, but I've got no one to blame but myself. I could still be flying old Sven Strnad's mail plane if I hadn't thought it was a fine idea to land downwind in a snowstorm on an unimproved strip. I remember thumping over a frozen field, a crumpled wingtip, snapped nose gear, mailbags in the snow.

Strnad had to let me go for insurance reasons, and that was it until Lambert called. He'd heard about the accident and wanted to run something past me. His second pilot had left for the airlines, and he wondered if maybe we could help each other out. I could pull the power back for a while, and he'd be off the hook, at least for the short term.

He wasn't being especially kind; that wasn't Roger Lambert. He was a pretty cold-fish man who never got too close to anybody that I ever saw. He did teach me to fly, though, and I'd worked for him before I'd left Maine.

Anyway, when I didn't answer right away, he made this little snort and said he hoped I wasn't still carrying a bloody torch. I knew he was talking about Katie Jones, who was this other girl I used to know.

"No" was all I said.

"Good," he said. "So, have you still got the one-eighty?"

"Yep," I said.

"Well, crank it up. I'll see you in a few days."

It was six o'clock in the morning when he hung up, but Dora was already outside, loading the feeders. I watched her slog back through the snow, her wild, thick hair pushed out around the parka hood. She'd tucked the bottom of her flannel nightgown into her boots. Her breath shot out in clouds. We'd been together a year; just one of those random things. Neither of us was any big prize, but we had our fun.

Dora stopped to fill the pole feeder and then came inside and saw me sitting at the table.

"You're up early," she said.

She took the parka off, ran her hands through her mass of red hair. Dora was as Irish as they come. I told her that once and she said, "Yeah—face like a potato."

"Don't run yourself down," I said, but she just laughed. The second time she said it, I carved a cute little face on a peeled potato and showed it to her.

"There you are," I said, and it felt pretty good when she threw her arms around my neck.

It didn't feel so good now, the way she was looking at me, and I finally told her I'd had an offer to go back to Maine and work.

She said, "Huh," pried her boots off, and went over to the woodstove.

"So, what do you think?" I said.

"Not up to me." She rubbed her hands together over the heat.

I'd fed it while she was outside. She took the percolator off the stove and poured herself a cup and sat down in the easy chair by the window.

"After I get squared away I can come back."

She laughed.

"Seriously," I said. Then I went over and took her hands, but she stood up and strode past me to the bedroom at the end of the trailer. She shut the door, and I couldn't decide whether it would be good to join her, so I poured another cup of coffee and sat down to think it over.

When she came out a half hour later she seemed fine.

Three days later she gave me a ride to the airstrip, helped me with the tie-downs, kissed me good-bye. Her lips were warm in the crackling cold. I guess it was about fifteen below.

I climbed aboard and got the 180 started and rumbled down the frozen airstrip between eight-foot snowbanks and lifted into the air.

When I banked back over the field I saw her: tiny, waving.

I bang the last ashtray top, drop it back onto its base.

When I go back behind the Avis counter, the kid says, "We a little cranky this morning?"

"Just bored."

I open the hard-covered Avis book to see what's up for the day. I lean close and squint; Lambert's handwriting isn't much better than the kid's. Doesn't look like much going on.

"I hear it used to be pretty exciting," the kid says, like he knows something.

"Spit it out," I say.

He laughs. "My mother was a bridesmaid."

"For real?"

"She's still mad you got her dress dirty."

I shut the Avis book and walk over to the window. It's brighter outside, and a breeze is lifting the wind sock. I remember flying toward the steeple, diving down at the wedding party.

"How come nobody turned you in, anyway?" the kid says.

"Maybe they tried. I didn't wait around."

He laughs, looks out the door. "Oops. Guess it's time."

I look at the parking lot. There are cars sitting with their engines running, exhaust curling up past the pole lights. There's a couple of Norm Lavin's taxis out there, too, waiting to see if anyone will need a ride when the plane comes in from Boston. That's all the little commuter does, round-trips between Boston and Baxter.

"Think you could take a swipe at my floor?" the kid says.

I go into the hangar for the mop, slap it over the tiles. The kid puts the slippery floor sign down and unlocks the door. The people start coming in and I take the mop back and stick it in its bucket and head for the 206 to preflight it for the day. The hell with old weddings, I think.

I find a nick on the three-bladed prop and take a moment to file it smooth. Then I open the cowling and turn petcocks, pull dip-sticks, check fluids. But my mind keeps going back to Katie—how she'd been working part-time for Lambert, renting cars, answering the phone—and how one day I got brave enough to ask if she'd like to go up for a little ride.

I wipe my hands on an old rag and go outside to have a cigarette.

I feel the damn ache all over again. She was so pretty it still killed me. I'd never had a really dazzling girlfriend, and that made it worse when she ditched me. It was like thinking you'd won the lottery, then finding out you'd written the goddamn number down wrong.

I light up, blow smoke toward the wind sock.

The owl hangs around; nobody scares him off, which is good, because it gives me something to think about besides failed flying careers, or old failed romances. It works sometimes, anyway.

Other times I can't help myself, like when I find out Katie and her husband bought the farmhouse out by the old quarry. I have to wonder if living there ever makes her think about me. See, we hung out there some. There was a sandy place behind an outcropping where we'd put a blanket down. I'd lay my hand on her ribs, move it up. She'd hold her breath. It got her going, making out in broad daylight, even if hardly anybody ever showed up besides us and the Russians who used to live over there.

But our big romance only lasted a couple of months. When I went to Florida to get my twin-engine rating, everything changed. Like, out of sight, out of mind. First, she stopped taking my calls at home. Then she quit work, so I couldn't call her there. Finally I got the note that said straight out she was now in love with Chris Cousins.

Not only that, they were getting married.

"I'm so sorry," she wrote. "It happened so fast. I'll always remember this summer, though."

How about that for a kick in the ass? I quit the course cold, checked out of the motel, and drove straight through to her parents' house, twenty-three hours. I banged on the door, but Katie wouldn't open it wide enough to let me come in.

"Oh, Russell," she said. "It's not like I planned it or anything."

"Chris Cousins?" I said. "The old used-car king?"

"He sells new cars, too," she said.

The family mutt tried to bust past her to see me, but she blocked him with her hip and closed the door so all I could see was her eyes and nose. I heard the mutt go clicking off over the hardwood floor.

"Are you going to dress up funny and go on TV with him?"

"Please don't be bitter."

"What did you expect?"

"I hoped we could still be friends."

I laughed. Then I shook my head.

"What the hell," I said. "When's the wedding?"

"Please, Russell," she said, and eased the door shut.

The next time I saw her was *at* the damn wedding. That was the last time, too.

At least it was memorable. Their little faces turned up like sunflowers, the minister first, then Katie and Chris Cousins looking over their shoulders, and then everybody else. Then they all hit the deck. I must have come within fifty feet of them before I banked up and around the church steeple and roared off down the river.

Shortly thereafter I started my little trek across the country, getting work here and there, leaving and moving on, heading west, finally making it all the way out to Alaska.

I never did get my twin rating.

The kid's young wife shows up one night. She blushes and looks down when he introduces us, before hustling her into the commuters' back room.

I sit down at my counter and listen to the metal Avis sign squeaking from its pole on the roof. It's gusty, and I wonder suddenly if the owl is okay. Then I wonder what exactly brought him here in the first place. Drought? Famine? Fire? A broken heart?

I laugh and walk over to the other side of the room and put my ear to the door. The kid's talking low to the girl.

I think about them getting married so young and wonder about Katie, who wasn't a whole lot older when she took up with Cousins. He had her by at least ten years, which was another thing I could never figure. It did me good to catch him on TV one night and see how his age was starting to show. He was sitting on an elephant, joking about trunk space, and he'd put on weight and his hair had thinned.

I still didn't get it. Katie loved to go flying with me. When it was nice we'd head down the river and swoop over the islands with their spiky firs and white beaches. The water would look like a heavy wet fabric in the sun. Katie would clap her hands at the view. But then I went to Florida, and she fell in love with Chris Cousins.

Maybe she just liked luxury sedans better than high-wing Cessnas.

I walk away from the kid's door and look through my reflection at the wind sock. I see the plowed runway and the snowbanks and the white fields and the trees. It looks like Alaska now even without the owl, and after a moment I wonder how old Dora's doing. I picture her stomping around the yard, feeding the birds, and after a bit I follow an impulse to give her a call and tell her about my visitor.

I forget that it's still the middle of the night in Nakasuk, but Dora never worried too much about sleep anyway.

I bring up the owl right away. "He's been around almost every day."

"Huh," she says. "Funny, I had one here too, but he took off."

"Maybe it's the same one."

"Well, listen," she says, "find your own damn owls."

I laugh. "How's everything else going?"

She briefs me on how so-and-so was back in jail. How such-and-such was running for state legislature. How what's-his-name married that Inuit girl he'd knocked up.

"And Strnad was asking about you," she says.

"Where'd you see him?"

"At the snowmobile race."

"What'd he want?"

"To see if you wanted to do some scenic flying."

"Kid stuff," I say.

"Different insurance, he says. It could get you going again, maybe."

"Maybe."

Then there's one of those awkward pauses.

"Well," I say, "probably should let you get back to sleep."

"Okay," she says.

"Good night, then."

"Don't work too hard."

We have some mild weather, but just when I'm starting to think about spring, a couple of storms blow through and knock us right back where we started. The snowbanks rise and the woods are deep and quiet.

At work things slow down to a crawl. There's still the commuter flights, though, and I empty the ashtrays and mop the floor and rent the occasional car. I prep the 206 for Lambert's charters and stay around to work the radio when he comes back late.

One morning he calls me at work and says, "So you comfortable flying the two-oh-six?"

"Got a thousand hours in them."

"I know, but you ain't flown them much lately."

"Because you're a stick hog."

"It's just that they're used to me."

"Whatever," I say. "I'm good to go."

"I don't need it racked up."

I don't even bother responding to that. Frigging Lambert.

"Okay, then," he says. "There's a trip popped up for this afternoon. I've got my father moving in with us today, and there's no way Susan can handle that by herself and watch Tomi and Little Roger at the same time."

"No sweat," I say. "Where am I going?"

"Portland," he says, and now there's something funny in his voice.

"What?" I say.

He laughs. "It's your old buddy."

I think a minute. "Cousins?"

"He's doing a new commercial down there. Can you handle it?"

"I can if he can."

After he hangs up I walk out from behind the counter and over to the window. It's gloomy and gray and looks like snow again. The owl's back on the pole, but he's lost some of his white because of the warm spell, and now he looks a little out of place.

"Chris Cousins," I say. "How about them apples?"

The owl ruffles his feathers, leans off the pole, and takes a turn over the field.

I imitate his flight with a hand, banking it through the lobby air, letting it lift and stall. I feel the kid watching from his counter, and can almost see him shaking his head and rolling his sleepy eyes.

At two o'clock I taxi the 206 out of the hangar. It's been snowing lightly, and I leave precise tracks on my way to the intersection. I thump down the runway, yank myself into the air, bank into a turn for Portland.

I'm in the stuff the whole way, flying instruments. It's a headwind, too, which slows everything down. Finally I descend into Portland, breaking out well above minimums. I land and taxi past the main terminal to the little brick General Aviation Terminal and see the bulky shape of Chris Cousins, standing at the edge of the ramp, hands in the pockets of his long coat.

Just as I cut the engine a woman walks out of the terminal to join him, all bundled up in a winter coat and hat. It's Katie. There's no mistaking her gait: slow, with her shoulders back, like she's inspecting the troops. I guess Lambert forgot to mention that she'd be coming along.

I take my headset off and hang it on the yoke, slide my seat back, pop the door, and climb out.

Cousins sees me and points, and they head over across the ramp.

Katie passes under the wing before she looks at me. Snowflakes are preserved on her black hat, and her cheeks are pink from the cold. She looks pretty nice; a bit of a double chin, some new crow's-feet, but nice. She looks good enough that my old heart starts to thump.

Her own gaze is friendly and impersonal; she's just looking because I'm not who she expected. Then her eyes open wide.

"Russell?" she says. "Oh my God!"

"Yeah," I say. "Lambert couldn't make it."

"I didn't even know you were back in town!"

"I've been trying to keep a low profile."

She laughs, puts her hands on her hips, and stares at me. Her pocketbook slides from her shoulder all the way down to her wrist.

She turns to Chris Cousins. "Do you have any idea who this is?"

Cousins makes a how-would-I-know face.

"This is Russell Barnes!"

Cousins still doesn't get it.

"Our wedding!" Katie says.

His eyebrows shoot up. "That was you?"

"Afraid so."

He looks at Katie and back at me. Then he grins.

"Well, what the hell," he says. "Long time ago. And we did get a good story out of it! Katie still tells everybody she meets about the poor brokenhearted pilot who buzzed our wedding!"

"I do not!" Katie says. But she smiles.

Cousins winks.

"It was pretty damn creative, at least. And you just did your thing and left, you didn't hang around like somebody else I could mention." He nudges Katie. "Remember the Swede, honey?"

"Oh, Lord," she says.

"Who's that?" I say.

"I forget his name. Some townie. Lumsden?"

"Lunden," Katie says.

"Yeah, Lunden, but we called him the Swede. Lived up over the hardware store. We'd see him looking out the window all the time. Rode this old Scout around. Katie was nice to him once or twice, and he never got over it. He'd sit across the road and watch the house. If we went somewhere, he'd follow. We'd look in the rear-view mirror and see that damn fool on his bike."

Suddenly I remember the Indian, coming out of Katie's road. An older guy, maybe Lambert's age. A guy I'd seen roaming around other places, one of those loser types you see in every small town. He'd give me a grin and a little salute as we passed one another, and I used to wonder about that.

"You sure could pick 'em, honey," Cousins says.

"Christopher," Katie says.

"Present company excluded!" Cousins says quickly.

"Don't worry about it." There's a gust and I feel snow on my face. I squint up into it. "Well," I say, "we should probably get moving."

"Is it bad?" Katie says.

"Just a little snowy."

"Is it going to get worse?"

"It's supposed to get better."

"Let's go, then," Cousins says. He wags a finger at me. "No dive-bombing, though!"

"You got it."

We all laugh very congenially and Katie holds out her hand. I take it and put my other hand on her back and brace her while she steps up into the plane. It takes a little more effort than I expected. But I get her in, and she squeezes behind the pilot's seat and moves over. Then Cousins grabs the strut and hauls himself up beside her.

I wait until they snake their seat belts into place, climb in, shut the door, and look over my shoulder.

"We ready?" I say.

"Roger Wilco!" Cousins says.

I fire up the engine, and as we taxi out toward the runway I go through the standard briefing about exits, seat belts, and unlikely events. I don't know if they're listening or not. I'm barely listening myself.

We're in the weather again and it's like the trip down: gloomy, a little bumpy, nothing but slanting snow. We drone along and I listen in the headset to Cousins and Mrs. Cousins talking about all the excitement they had in the big city. I keep an eye on the instruments and think back about Katie and me.

I think about our brief romance and the letter I got, and remember how I drove straight through to try and talk her out of getting married. I remember the poor dumb mutt who still loved me. And then buzzing the goddamn wedding.

I realize that it doesn't feel quite so devastating anymore. I think about the Swede and the two of us coming and going, and Cousins lurking around, and who knows who else, and my perspective keeps shifting until it actually starts to hit me funny. I mean, here we all are now, jammed into this little Cessna! I think about shoving Katie up into the plane, and Cousins squeezing in beside her, and the old Swede riding around somewhere with her initials probably tattooed on his ass.

Right after that's when we bust out on top of the clouds. We're sailing along through bright sunshine under a brilliant blue sky, with the clouds rolling away beneath us like snow-covered foothills. A few minutes later they start to break up too, and I can see the pine forest encircling white meadows and stark little towns.

I smile back at my passengers and point out the window. I give them a thumbs-up and turn back to the yoke, and after a bit I'm close enough to Baxter to call in on the Unicom frequency.

The kid answers, sounding sleepy as always. "Nobody's talking. I guess it's all yours."

"How about the owl?" I say.

"He's not talking either."

"You're funny," I say. "Seriously, is he around?"

"Ain't seen him all day."

"Good," I say. "Ten minutes out."

"Roger Lambert," he says, and we both laugh.

I swing into a turn over the bay and fly up the river. It narrows under me and twists and turns through the woods. I line up over Primus Blake's old red-roofed barn and head northwest, and thirty seconds later pick up the runway, an incongruously straight swath through the trees west of town. I pull back the power and take us on down.

On short final I look around for the old boy, but he's nowhere to be seen. Just in case, though, I touch down at the very end of the runway: a perfect soft landing.

"Nice job," Cousins says through the headset.

We taxi in to the terminal and park in front of the hangar, and I get out and chock the nose wheel.

Cousins grunts, wriggling out of the backseat. Katie holds her hand out and he takes it this time and helps her thump down. Then they both turn and look at me.

"It was nice to see you again, Russell," Katie says.

"It was lovely," I say.

"No hard feelings, eh?" Cousins says.

"Nary a one."

Cousins smiles and takes Katie's arm. She flutters her fingers at me and they turn and walk toward the terminal, Katie with her slow general's gait, Cousins sort of waddling beside her. I feel the smile stretching back onto my face, and I watch until they've gone through the fence gate into the parking lot. Then I march over to the hangar door.

Inside I go to the workbench, check my watch, pick up the phone.

"Hey, Potato Face," I say when she answers.

It's just before dawn on the morning I leave. We've had a week of thaw and the snow's all melted away. Roger Lambert helps push the 180 out of the hangar and tries one last time to get me to stay on. I tell him I'm sorry to leave him in the lurch, but I just can't do anything about it right now.

"Tell me it's not that Katie Jones business," he says.

"Not the way you think."

He shakes his head and limps out of the way. I look into the lobby, see the kid watching through the plate-glass window. I give him a salute, climb into the craft, and fire up the engine. It roars and smooths, and I feel the slight lift of its backwash.

I nod to Lambert and motor out, watching the rpms and the oil, setting the altimeter. I swing onto the centerline, check how the compass lines up. Everything's perfect, and I make my call and push in the throttle. I feel a bump, the tail lifts, trees blur by. I pass the wind sock and nose away from the ground and I'm free, rising and dipping a wing to turn. I cross the river and swing back over the town. I come around past the steeple, head her northwest and look down at my shadow, fluttering over the landscape below.

Roger Jr.

Roger Jr.'s grandfather never said a word until they passed the lot where the old train station was coming down. Then he leaned sideways and snapped, "*Arrêtez!*" so abruptly and commandingly that Junior's father hit the brakes. Tires screeched behind them and he quickly took his foot off the brake and yanked them over to the curb.

A Buick skinned past with a woman's red face in its window. Junior's father threw the gearshift into park and stared straight ahead.

"It's all right, Roger," Junior's mother said.

His father kept staring. Junior could hear him breathing.

Beside Junior the old man pointed shakily at the lot, where a big wrecking crane was slinging a heavy leaden ball into the clock tower.

"*Là-bas!*" the old man said. He never spoke English anymore.

Junior's father worked the gearshift and pulled ahead, so they were better aligned against the curb. There was a bang and everybody looked as the clock tower fell in on itself.

"Cool!" Junior said. He never saw stuff like this in Baxter.

The crane gathered itself for another heavy blow. Its ball swung forward and more stone fell, but not nearly as impressively as the tower with the clock. *"Je veux voir!"* the old man said.

Junior's parents got out. They met at the back of the wagon and worked together to lift the wheelchair free, spreading its armrests until they clicked into place. Then Junior's father pushed the chair along the brick sidewalk. He bent down and locked the wheels.

"Slide out," he said to Junior.

They helped his grandfather onto the sidewalk, where he stood unsteadily, staring at what was left of the stone building. Junior noticed his grandfather's patchy complexion and the cowlick in his white hair and the way his hands trembled.

"Can I push?" he said.

"I'll do it," his father said.

"Let him help, Roger," Junior's mother said.

"All right, then. Come on, Papa. Junior will take you over for a look."

They eased him down onto the canvas seat of the chair.

"Je veux aller!" the old man said.

Junior leaned against the chair, rolling it along the sidewalk. It was noisy with the crane working and the loaders scooping up stone fragments and dumping them into the shaking trucks. The demolition ball seemed to pause on impact and then push slowly into the stone. He watched closely, shoving the chair along. Behind him his father said he couldn't believe the goddamn station was coming down today, of all days.

"Isn't it always the way?" Junior's mother said.

The dump trucks rumbled past, and Junior's father called for them to come back.

"It's too dusty for you, Papa," he said, crouching at eye level with Junior's grandfather. When the old man didn't respond, he put his hands on his thighs and straightened to look at his son. "It's just that this place meant a lot to your grandfather."

Junior squinted at the ruins. "How come?"

"You've heard the story," Junior's father stated, and Junior realized then what all this was about: the legend of his grandfather's return from the Great War, and how he'd met Junior's grandmother.

This was the exact place!

He *had* heard the story, several times, of how his grandmother, Marie Carrièr, a Maine French from Lewiston, had been waiting for hours in the station, and how she'd stamped her foot and cried *Òu es-tu!* when her missing soldier wasn't among the troops that got off his grandfather's train, either.

And he'd heard how his grandfather, whose parents spoke French at home, had stopped to strike up a halting *conversation en français* with the young lady—not wolfishly (he was shy around women), but out of a sort of tribal concern. And of course it wouldn't have become a legend if things hadn't gone on from there, so that by the time the next train chuffed up to the station they had managed to fall head over heels in love.

The tale always ended with the two of them hurrying out of the station before any more passengers debarked, in case Marie Carrièr's missing beau walked through the door and complicated things at the last minute.

Junior looked at the battered train station, at the huge clock in the rubble.

He let go of the wheelchair and stepped to the side, pretending to stretch, angling to peek at the old man, and thought for a moment that he saw something telltale in the worn face, something revealing about the train station and his youth and all that had happened to him.

But it didn't last long enough for Junior to be sure.

A large, flat section of wall collapsed. Junior's grandfather tried to look, but Roger Lambert wouldn't move out of the way.

"What if you fell again, Papa?" he said, "and I wasn't home to help you back up?"

The old man leaned the other way and craned his neck.

"All right," Junior's father said. "I'm sorry. We have to go."

Junior pushed his grandfather back, noting the soft sound the wheels made on the bricks. His parents helped his grandfather into the car and wrestled the chair into the back. Then Junior got in beside the old man and they set off again, driving away from the demolition and up to the high-arcing bridge, crossing the wide river. Far below them an old barge moved ponderously upstream past the oil tank farms.

When they got back to Portland the sun had set, turning the water black. Up ahead lights were coming on in the hilly city.

"Grandpa didn't like it there one bit," Junior said.

His grandfather's new home was in an old gabled house that was bright and clean inside, and at first, Junior had thought it was nice. But the room was divided by a curtain, behind which another elderly man had coughed and muttered the whole time they were there. Junior hadn't liked that so much, and neither had his grandfather, judging from the way he'd sat glumly while they'd moved his belongings in.

"He'll be okay, though," Junior's father said.

"Once he adjusts," his mother added.

They swung onto St. John Street, rode along the foot of Western Promenade.

When they stopped at the Congress Street intersection, Junior walked on his knees across the backseat to where his grandfather had sat on the way out. He looked at the lot where the old station had stood. It was mostly gone now, and the tracks behind it showed up clearly.

He thought about the train pulling in and his grandfather shouldering his duffel bag, jumping down from the steps, and walking into the station. He thought about the young woman waiting alone, and how his grandfather had spoken to her in French.

Then he thought about them falling in love, and hearing the train whistle, and hurrying out so nothing would stop them from staying together forever.

He thought about his grandmother dying before he was born, and an entirely different sort of feeling struck him. Junior looked at the dark lot and the feeling struck him again, so that it shook him inside. The light changed then and they started across the intersection, but he wasn't ready to look away just yet.

He pressed his cheek against the window to keep the old station in view. It seemed high-minded to do so, and he'd never felt that way about anything before. They kept moving and he crawled into the way-back, to make it last a little longer. For at least another minute he watched cars coming off the Veterans Bridge throw complicated shadows behind the Union Station ruins.

Larry

It's my stepbrother, Lucas, who calls to tell me. I'm in Palo Alto and he's still in Baxter, but we've kept in touch over the years.

Lucas says he has bad news. He says last night the old man went outside for a stroll on the desert but never made it off the boardwalk. Our mother saw the whole thing from the desk in the gift shop: how he grabbed at his forehead, staggered a few feet, and pitched facedown into the zinnias. She called the fire station, and the ambulance got there pretty fast and somebody jumped out and tried mouth-to-mouth, but it was too late; the old man was already gone.

"So what's the *bad* news?" I say.

"Come on, Larry," Lucas says, and something in his voice—it's so *little brother* all at once—takes me right back. I see the eagle-eyed old man at the register. I see Lucas filling souvenir jars with colored sand. I see our mother at the snack-bar grill, and my sixteen-year-old self, leading a family of tourists out onto the desert. None of that changes my reaction much.

"Larry?" Lucas says again.

"All right," I say. "I'll come back."

❧

Lucas never really understood how it was for me. When I finally worked up the nerve to escape, he actually tried to talk me out of it. I remember we took one last walk on the desert while he gave it his best shot. But the next morning I was gone, just like I'd promised. And I stayed gone, too. Sometimes, talking to him or our mother on the phone, I'd get a little homesick for them and for Baxter, and even for the desert in a funny way.

But never for that old man. Because of him I kept moving, until eventually I'd put a whole continent between us.

See, I was the stepson, and he was a jealous man, and that made all the difference. I would always be a constant reminder that his wife had not only loved someone else, but had also managed to reproduce with him. And not only that, but had whelped a pansy, a kid who turned out to be a living insult to generations of steadfast and manly Hurds.

I understood this on some level when I was very young, and it makes me cringe to this day to remember my attempts to change into someone the old man might find acceptable. It was almost comical, I suppose. But after a few days of walking bowlegged and scratching my privates and spitting, of throwing rocks and cussing and otherwise imitating my far more stalwart stepbrother, I'd somehow always forget myself, and then old man Hurd would catch me skipping down the boardwalk singing "Over the Rainbow" or some such nonsense, and we'd be right back to square one.

If, indeed, he'd noticed my pathetic efforts in the first place.

❧

After Lucas says good-bye I call my boss and tell her I'll need a couple of days off. Sandra is a typical restaurant manager in many ways, but can still muster a bit of humanity now and then, and after she goes on for a while about losing her sous chef with Easter coming up, it crosses her mind to ask if something might have happened.

"Well," I say, "my stepfather has died."

"Oh, Lawrence!" she says. "I'm so sorry!"

"We weren't that close."

I carry the phone over to the window, look out at the President Hotel. I can't quite see the restaurant behind the palmettos and palms along the street, but I know Sandra is already hard at work on the evening's specials.

"It's all about family, at this point," I tell her, because that sounds like something you would say.

"Oh, honey," Sandra says. "Of course."

Next I call the theater. I'm only crew for the current production, so that's no big deal. Finally, I leave a message on Jeffrey's voice mail, just in case he decides to get in touch. I doubt that will happen, since the last time we were together he told me I had a barren, godforsaken heart and he never wanted to see me again.

But you never know, do you?

The next morning I'm in line at SFO. The line moves slowly around stanchions and ropes, and I have time to think about home, about walking tourists around the desert, doing my family job, even enjoying it in some ways: my first taste of performing, after all.

I remember some of the people clearly, like the man I thought was Bobby Kennedy but who changed the subject when I asked, and the kid from Madawaska who fell down the dune and sprained his ankle, and how he leaned on me when I helped him, and looked at me when we were back at the top, and how his pretty eyes made me feel.

Of course I hated the feeling, and when I was back in the gift shop I made sure to point out the sissy kid walking to the parking lot with his parents, and to tell the old man how he'd carried on like a baby over a little sprained ankle.

"You're one to talk," was what the old man said back.

There's no direct connection from out west to the little Baxter airport, so I have to fly into Portland. It's three hours, and I'm stiff and tired when we finally arrive. I trudge through the terminal and outside to the curb, looking for points of reference that will feel like home. But there's really nothing that stands out. People seem overdressed and buttoned up, for April. That's about it.

I find my way out of the new airport grid to the 295 ramp. They've redone the highway since I've been away. It's smooth and dark now, with mirage puddles on the crests of its hills. I scoot past Portland on the bypass and head up the coast. I can't find a radio station I like, but it only takes me a half hour to get to the billboard, right where it's always been:

> COME VISIT THE SAHARA OF MAINE!
> EIGHTH WONDER OF THE WORLD!
> THOMAS HURD, PROP.

The sign features a camel and two smiling boys. One is a dirty blond, like I was, and the other, dark like Lucas, but that's where the resemblance ends. We were never that carefree.

My first job was wiring bumper signs onto the cars in the parking lot. We never asked permission, but nobody minded, and sometimes they even tipped me. I hoarded that money and made more when Lucas took over the bumper signs and I became a desert guide.

The tours lasted an hour, and I would chatter the whole time about the history of the old property: how it had been a farm, how the topsoil had eroded and had exposed the huge glacial deposit lurking beneath. I would tell how the prevailing winds had spread the sand to the river, and point out the buried springhouse, where you could still lower a bucket and bring up sweet, cold water. I would "find" natural glass, where lightning had fused the sand, and lead them to patches of brilliant colors, where the sand had been stained by decayed plants and, possibly, animals. This very same sand, I'd be sure to tell them, was used in the sand jars that were on sale in the gift shop.

The sand jars were a hot item, thanks to Lucas. The old man had conceived of layering the colored sand into jars and selling them, but Lucas had taken it about a dozen steps further. He'd figured out how to make little scenes and landscapes that were actually quite beautiful.

Lucas could do nearly anything with sand.

I ramp off the highway and head down the Desert Road, passing signs with red Arabic-like lettering: *Two more miles to the Sahara of Maine! One more mile to the Sahara of Maine!* And it's exactly one mile later that I round a curve and see the gift shop and the barn and the stockade fence. The fence was there so people couldn't see the desert without paying. Thomas Hurd didn't give anything away—not to customers . . . not even to his family.

He was the sheik in his little desert kingdom, and we were all his subjects.

"I run a tight caravan!" was his definitive, barked joke. He meant it, too. Nothing was free; wives were meant to serve the needs of the family; kids were to be seen and not heard. He issued commands that he didn't want to have to say twice, always on the alert for goldbricking or carelessness.

Old Thomas kept everyone on a pretty short leash, but naturally mine was the shortest. He never locked me in a closet and fed me dog food or anything like that, but it could get cumulative and dicey. I remember one evening when the mere sight of me sitting at the table, waiting for supper with my legs crossed and my hands in my lap—and, I must assume, a faggy look on my face—infuriated him to the point where he yanked me out of my seat and told me to leave unless I thought I could sit like a goddamn boy.

He would have said more, but I started howling. He'd managed to dislocate my elbow and it hurt like blazes. When they realized I was actually injured and not just being a crybaby, they took me into town to the clinic, where the on-call doctor worked my arm like a pump shotgun to get everything back into alignment—something that still makes me queasy to think about—and where, when the old man lied about roughhousing and I gaped at my mother in outrage, she made it clear with a look that I was not to contradict him. (Later, after I figured out how badly I was being treated—but before I understood that she was a victim, too—that earned her the number-two spot on my shit list.)

The old man did apologize on the way home, though. He said, "I'm sorry you made me do that," which is what he always said.

Lucas and I had long before made a joke out of it: One of us would sneak up on the other and slug him, or snap an ear, and as long as the statement "I'm sorry you made me do that" followed quickly enough, there could be no retaliation. One time Lucas caught me with a titty-twister right in front of the old man, and I remember his puzzled look after I whirled around to slap Lucas and he froze me by saying the magic words. Old Hurd wasn't an imaginative or inquisitive sort of guy; he just shook his head and said, "Knock it off, you two," and went back to whatever he'd been doing.

Lucas and I ran up to our bedroom and shut the door and Lucas leaned against it, laughing through his hand.

Our bedroom was right over the gift shop.

Every summer morning before daybreak the old man would bellow, "Rise and shine!" up the stairway, and we'd roll out and go downstairs, tucking in our Sahara of Maine T-shirts. He'd already be running a mop over the floor, rearranging the stuffed camels on the shelves, counting out the cash drawer. We'd eat our cereal and drink our juice and Lucas would get the bowls of colored sands and the jars and utensils out. I'd sweep the boardwalk and open the guide house—a tiny, renovated chicken coop—and stand ready to meet the tourists where the boardwalk began.

There's a scaled-down version of the highway billboard over the gift shop door, and I blow those boys a kiss as I walk up, just for old times' sake. I really can't believe I'm back. It seems surreal.

I open the door and walk past shelves of stuffed camels, little plastic pyramids, T-shirts, and caps. Sand jars and tubes of lightning-glass, rough on the outside, glazed on the inside; SAHARA OF MAINE pennants. Then I reach the end of the aisle and see Lucas himself, sitting at the same old workbench under a hanging light, using a long-handled scoop to drop sand into a jar. He's grown into a big, rangy guy, a lot like the old man. He glances up at me and his eyes open wide. He holds up a finger, squints, drops another bit of sand. I walk over to have a look. It's a desert scene, and he's working on the sky, with gulls. Gulls are easy—just shallow Vs—something even I could do. But I was never any good at the more-difficult stuff.

"Very nice," I say.

"I could do this in my sleep."

"So where's Mother?"

"She's been lying down every afternoon."

"Did she know I was coming?"

"I figured I'd wait until you actually showed up."

Lucas doesn't take his eyes off the jar. He pours a fine stream of plain sand into the middle, pushes it around with the hull of the scoop. Then he gently puts the jar into a wooden holder, where it sits with two others, each nestled upright through two holes. He dusts his hands together and says, "Okay. So, welcome home."

He stands up and we think about hugging each other. We shake hands instead.

"You want some coffee?"

"Don't mind if I do."

He takes me out the side door. We go into the snack bar and I get all kinds of childhood vibes. They still have the four-chambered drink machine: pink and regular lemonade, grape juice, orange juice. Beside it is a shiny new coffeemaker. Lucas pours two cups, slides mine forward.

"So," he says, "you married yet?"

"Haven't found the right girl."

We laugh; it's one of our long-running jokes, something he told Mother whenever she raised the question. Lucas himself is divorced. He has two daughters, living with his ex-wife, and he's moved back in at the Sahara. But he's been working there all along. I try to imagine sticking around like he did, with that old man.

I put my coffee down and look at Lucas and he smirks back at me, like he's reading my mind. He probably is; we were always pretty tuned in, for stepbrothers. We were more tuned in than I ever was with anyone else, even Jeffrey, I'd have to say.

The night I ran off Lucas woke as soon as I climbed down from the upper bunk. He propped his head on his hand, watched me get dressed.

Then he whispered, "Are you really leaving?"

I reached under my mattress, pulled out the bus ticket.

A couple of days before, the old man had caught me in the guide house practicing a dance move—a sort of elbows-at-the-waist gyration, like swiveling while holding a bag of feed, that I'd admired during a few stolen minutes watching *American Bandstand*—and his reaction, besides the usual look of aversion, had been to say, "There's plenty to do around here if you've got all that energy to burn," and to push me toward the gift shop and direct me into a series of chores: brooming the boardwalk, raking the parking lot smooth, and cleaning the restroom. This was far from the worst I'd ever been treated, but for some reason, it clinched a decision to leave.

Straw and camel's back, I guess. Hardy-har.

The next Saturday when he rode into Baxter to do his errands, I jumped into the back of his pickup. He saw me, but didn't care enough to do anything about it. When he stopped at the town garage to try and sell them sand for winter—he tried every year, but always wanted too much—I waited until he went inside, then raced down to the drugstore and bought the ticket.

When I got back I saw him outside, talking to a tall, bleary-looking guy leaning on a shovel by a pile of crushed rock. My step-father was back-to, waving his arms and complaining—he'd struck out again, apparently—and I remember how the tall guy looked past him at me and covertly raised an eyebrow, like he knew I'd been up to something, but would keep it between the two of us.

It surprised me, and gave me a little boost, somehow.

Anyway, Lucas looked the ticket over, then handed it back.

He seemed sad, so I said, "Secret walk?"

Nighttime walks on the desert were another part of our private existence, and I had the idea that it would help him if we did it one last time. He rolled out of his bed and got dressed. We climbed out the window and stole along the ridgepole of the snack bar. We stepped into an apple tree, monkeyed down its branches, and sneaked out the boardwalk, stopping for a drink at the springhouse.

"I can't believe you're actually leaving."

It was after midnight, the moon up bright, shadows from the trees stretching along the sand.

"Yes, sir," I said.

"Are you ever coming back?"

"No, sir."

"What about Mother?"

"She lets him get away with it."

The moon went behind a cloud and it got darker. The trees disappeared and we could have been in the actual Sahara, miles of sand around us. We marched on—Lucas taller than me, as he had been for a couple of years—until his breath caught and he sat down and let the sand run through his fingers. Then he put his hands on his knees.

"I'll keep in touch," I told him.

He was blinking like crazy.

"You can come and visit."

His face crumpled then, and I turned my back. When I faced him again his cheeks were all wet.

"Don't be a sissy," I said: a last tough-guy moment.

He stood up and gave me a shove. I pushed him back and we headed off the way we'd come. We passed the springhouse, walked down the boardwalk, and climbed the apple tree. In our bedroom we solemnly shook hands. He crawled into bed and watched me pack clothes and a library book I hadn't finished and intended to steal. At the window I looked back, and he was still watching, just his eyes showing above the blanket.

I always felt there was something I should have said, then. But I climbed out and set off along the Desert Road. I hiked all the way down to Route 1. The sky was just starting to lighten over the trees when the Greyhound came along, I flagged it down, and gave my ticket to the sleepy old driver.

"Where we off to, son?" he said.

"Portland." It was as far as I could afford to go. Far enough, it turned out. Nobody bothered to come after me, which was good, because I didn't get out west until a year later. I wound up in Arizona, got my GED, worked at a Holiday Inn. Saved for a few months, hit the road for the coast.

And now, I think, here I am, all the way back.

❦

Lucas takes me back through the gift shop, nods toward the hallway.

"She'll snooze all afternoon."

He opens the door and I follow him outside and look at the picnic tables, the guide house, the boardwalk. Everything's the same, but it seems smaller. Lucas nods toward the desert.

"Secret walk?"

I grin and follow him out onto the sand. Old guide phrases drift into my mind; it's amazing how much of that stuff sticks with you. We pass the springhouse, Lucas walking with his head down, kicking sprays of sand ahead. We scuff toward the dune and the edge of the woods and the river. The desert feels small to me, too, which is funny. In my mind it was always this vast barrens, fringed with greenery. Now, walking through it, my main impression is of an arid patch in the middle of the forest.

"I hated it when you left, you know," Lucas says then.

I don't say anything back. What can I say?

We cross to the dune and look down at the Baxter River. It's narrow up this way, high-banked and turbulent with spring runoff. I think about the kid who hurt himself, blubbering down by the water, leaning against me when I helped him to the top, and I wonder where he is now and whether he ever figured himself out.

Lucas steps closer and puts an arm around my shoulder.

It catches me by surprise. We Hurds were never much for touching. But then I realize he's not giving me an awkward sort of hug; he's just getting a grip. I don't catch on quickly enough, though. Before I can react he pivots and slings me right over the edge of the dune. I stumble and trip and lurch into this sort of downhill run and only manage to stay out of the river by throwing myself down and digging in with both hands.

I lie there hugging the desert, my heart thumping in my chest.

Then I get to my feet and brush myself off. I spit sand and glare up at Lucas, who's looking down at me with his hands on his knees. He's laughing, his shoulders shaking, and I growl and charge back up the slope. The dune shifts under me and I slip and slide, but finally make it to the top. I'm still pretty worked up, and I slog toward him with bad intentions.

But he just grins and holds up a hand.

"I'm sorry you made me do that," he says, and I'm sure he expects me to stop. Only, I don't. Oh, he's set me up perfectly, and I can't help but admire him for it, but that doesn't mean I have to play by those old rules anymore. When he gets what's happening, his eyes widen.

"Hey!" he says, just before I tackle him.

We wrestle until he finally throws me off. Then we face one another, sitting on our heels, panting. We're disheveled and red-faced and covered with sand, and it strikes us both funny at the same time.

Lucas cackles and slaps his hands down on his thighs.

I shake my head so that sand flies out of my hair.

He points and snorts and we giggle like fools.

Finally Lucas struggles to his feet and offers me a hand. He yanks me up and we slap the sand off our clothes and wipe our noses on our sleeves and call each other misanthropic names. Then we set off across the desert.

Halfway back he slings an arm around my shoulders—for real, this time—and I resist an impulse to shrug it away. We take small, uneven steps toward the farm, and just as we get to the boardwalk my eyes get damp and I think, Oh, Jeffrey, you ought to see me now.

Arnold

Usually I try to sit by Rocky Marciano, but today somebody beat me to it. So I end up by the kitchen, next to old Mysterious Billy Smith.

I'd never heard of Mysterious Billy until I came back to town and saw him on the restaurant wall. And he was a Baxter boy, too; I guess it just goes to show you. He looks like a fighter. He's got the busted nose, the kiss-my-ass eyes. He's bare-knuckled and wearing those tights they fought in way back, and he has his dukes up like he means business. Under his signature it says welterweight champion of the world, 1892. Imagine that.

I check the Rocky booth again. They're smiling at each other, a couple of swanks, probably trust-funders from Camden. They've got the look, anyway: sleek and sweatless. The guy holds up his hands peekaboo-style and dodges his head around, and the girl laughs. She's wearing this beret and her cheeks are rosy and her eyes are bright, and I feel a pang because I'm not the one she's smiling at.

Fat chance of that, I think.

While I'm watching an old-timer stops and looks in their window. He takes his skully off and pushes long gray hair behind his ears and squints into the restaurant, and that's when I realize it's none other than my old promoter, Sam Silverman. There's only one reason he'd ever show up in Baxter, and I go ahead and raise my hand. He grins, slaps the cap back, and disappears.

A few seconds later he comes shuffling past Muhammad Ali, Earnie Shavers, and Roberto Durán and stands beside the booth, looking at me with his usual shit-eating grin.

"Look what the cat dragged in," I say.

Silverman wags his head at the empty seat.

"Knock yourself out."

He drops into the seat without further ado, as the swanks might say. The old boy hasn't changed a lot. He's still big and beefy and dresses like a lumberjack, which I must say fits pretty well out here in the hinterlands.

"I hear you're driving an oil truck," he says.

"Just for the fun of it."

He laughs and looks around at all the signed pictures on the walls: Floyd Patterson, Preacher Lewis, Jerry Quarry. Sonny Liston, Vito Antuofermo, Marvin Hagler. That strange kid they called The Pink Cat, who fought a couple of times in Portland before he hit the skids.

Over the years Alva Potter has managed to get signed pictures from pretty much everybody. He even has Terry Hitchcock over by the door, a guy I fought twice, someone who did pretty well for a Maine kid—not up there with Mysterious Billy, maybe, but someone who actually got ranked for a couple of years.

I've joked with Alva about bringing one of mine in.

"So do it," he says in the tough-guy way he favors. But I haven't so far.

Silverman looks at the swanks in the Rocky booth and grunts.

"So what brings you to town?" I say.

"You're kidding, right?"

He spreads his hands on the table. He was a fighter, too, before he was a promoter. You can still see it in his ugly knuckles. He looks at something over my shoulder and I turn and see Tomi Lambert walking up, holding her order pad. Or Tomi Hurd, I guess her name is, even though I understand she divorced old Lucas a few years back.

Tomi's the main reason I've been hanging out here—not that I have any delusions. It's just nice to have someone like her waiting on me and being somewhat friendly.

"Yours is coming right up, Arnold," she says, and looks at Silverman.

"I'm in training." He winks at her.

Tomi smiles and heads off again. I watch her cross the room, as pretty as when she was a little girl, even tired out like she must be from working and raising a couple of kids on her own. She's told me it isn't easy finding someone when you're single with a couple of kids, but I'd definitely take a shot if I thought there was a snowball's chance. But to her I'm probably still the kid who tried to shoot his aunt and uncle, who got sent away to the State Farm for Boys until he turned eighteen.

And I doubt she's very impressed by my subsequent boxing career, because I never was a big name or anything. I was what they call an "opponent," the guy they call on short notice who'll put up a good-enough fight so the fans won't feel disappointed, but not so good that he might actually win. The kind of fighter the golden boys fatten their records on. I didn't *plan* on being that kind of fighter; that's just how it worked out.

"Speaking of training," Silverman says now.

"Gave it up for Lent."

"I was just gonna say, you don't look all that bad."

"Don't even bother, Sam."

I take another look at the Rocky booth. They're sipping their pints. I wonder again what they're doing in here, and then I get generous and think that maybe they're actual boxing fans. They can crop up anywhere, even in Camden.

"They been holding those amateur things at the Expo," Silverman says.

"I don't get to Portland that much."

"Just as well," he says. "It'd be an insult to a real fighter."

I laugh to show him I know where he's going.

It doesn't slow him down any.

"Anyway, I figure if they'll pay good money to see firemen and cops, they'll pay more to see the real thing. It won't be nothing fancy, four fight under card and a main. It ain't gonna be no blimp fight, that's for damn sure."

He pops his knuckles and smiles. I know he's working me, but my mind still goes right on back to when Georgie D'Amico took us to Atlantic City to watch a couple of up-and-comers. That was before I'd become an "opponent." I remember looking at the Goodyear Blimp all lit up in the sky, and then back at the fighters in the outdoor ring, and feeling like anything in the world was possible.

"Terry Hitchcock's signed up," Silverman says.

"*Now* I get it."

Silverman grins. "You'd make some decent dough."

"Sorry, Sam."

He sighs dramatically, then shrugs and pushes himself out of the booth.

"Just think about it, okay? That's all I ask."

He turns to go but spots the Mysterious Billy portrait on the wall and stops.

"Ever hear of him?" I say.

"Sure," he says. "Hell, I even met him one time, way back."

"No fooling?"

"I was just a kid, training for a fight. He was living in Portland then, an old soldiers' home up on the Hill. He was a vet of some kind. Anyway, I was running through the park and he was sitting on a bench, down by the duck pond. Suit and tie, even in August. He had some fussy nurse with him. I recognized him right off, could tell by the beak."

He moves his hand to show how Mysterious Billy's nose went in about four different directions.

"He must have been ninety and then some."

"Did you talk to him at all?"

"Oh yeah, I stopped and said hello. He could tell I was a fighter, not just somebody out for a jog. He said, 'Chin down, gloves up!' He had some big hands on him for a little guy."

"What was so mysterious about him?"

"I never figured that one out."

Silverman is still looking at the picture. "He stood up and made like he was throwing body shots. For a minute there he looked pretty serious. His nurse told him to take it easy. I said good-bye and ran off. Only saw him that once. I think he went down for the count not long afterwards." Silverman shakes his head, then looks back at me. "I almost forgot: Hitchcock said to say he was thinking of you."

"That's just plain sweet."

Sam laughs.

I think, Hitchcock—the only guy in the world who could strut doing roadwork. I picture him jogging through the park like the toughest guy in the world: bowlegged, chest out, arms swinging.

Not that he wasn't tough.

Silverman sticks a business card into my shirt pocket. "Call me if you change your mind." Then he shuffles off.

I watch him go out the door and then past the Rocky window. The swanks look at him and he tips his cap. They laugh as he disappears and I sit back and shake my head.

The old bastard's got me thinking, just like he intended.

I could definitely use the dough, with my mother in the nursing home, which is what brought me back to Baxter in the first place. And it's not like I have any deep hatred of fighting; it brought a bit of discipline into my life while I was still at the Farm, and kept me more or less on the straight and narrow after I got out.

There was a time when I thought it would do more than that, too. When Silverman showed up with D'Amico to watch me train, I thought that meant I was going places. When D'Amico invited me to the camp, I was sure of it. And you know, that feeling never completely died. Not when I found out I'd have to fight my way through the camp, or that I'd have to be twice as good as the kids coming out of Golden Gloves and AAU. Not even after I became an opponent. Hell, even now, there's a part of me that thinks I could still do it.

Talk about mysterious.

Tomi Lambert comes up and puts my plate down, then looks at her watch.

"Mind if I get off my feet for a second?"

"Not at all."

She sits down. "It's better if I stay near the kitchen."

"Makes sense."

"Who was your friend, Arnold?"

"Oh, a guy I knew."

"From boxing?"

"Yeah."

"I thought so. You're not fighting again."

"I told him no."

"Good for you."

Then somebody shouts her name, and she rolls her eyes and goes through the swinging door beside the bar into the kitchen. It's gotten busy, and I know they need the table, so I finish my meat loaf and beer, pay Potter at the register, and head outside.

I'm thinking about the Catskills, now, and I remember running on the pine needles before dawn, weight training until my arms went shaky, skipping rope and thumping the big bag, working on muscle memory: jab and step, hook and duck. Between that and fighting twice a week, they got me into great shape. That was the bad part when I quit: Training on my own just wasn't the same. I kept fighting, though, got by on what the *Portland Press Herald* called "a hard head and a big heart," made some money, lived it up for a few years. I can't help wondering what I might have done. I still made something of a name for myself; otherwise, why would Silverman come down to Baxter looking for me?

"Answer me that," I say out loud.

I've crossed the Speedway and the bridge and am driving down the River Road. It's November, and hunters are walking the roadside in their red flannel, rifles over their shoulders. The sun is already setting behind the trees over by the airport. I watch it sink all the way down, and by the time it disappears I'm turning into the lot where we keep the tanker truck.

❧

My first delivery is on the other side of town, out by the quarry, in this development they put up a few years ago in the old hayfield. A guy goes trotting past, running pretty smooth, and I think about Silverman running in the park, meeting Mysterious Billy. It's strange to think of him still being alive. That would have to have been in the 1940s. I can imagine Silverman stopping to talk, reaching his fists out, Billy tapping them with his own, both of them knowing to do it, like a secret handshake for some club. Then Sam jogging away with his arms flicking out in those fake roadwork punches. I think that it *is* sort of a club. We all share the history: roadwork, shadowboxing, training. Depriving ourselves. Climbing into the ring and risking our lives.

Some club, I think.

I get out of the truck, walk the hose to the inlet pipe, pull the trigger, and let it flow. I'm back to wishing I'd stuck out the camp, really just holding the idea in my mind, like I've done before any number of times. Suppose I'd managed to turn into one of those golden boys. I might've made some serious money. More than some, maybe, being white and all.

I never said it was an especially *fair* sort of club, you know?

I remember one of D'Amico's trainers named Walter Coombs, who fought for fifteen years and never got anywhere. He was pretty good, too, at least the way he tells it. He was wielding the paddles one day, taking me through different combinations, spinning tales about how they'd ducked him because he was too dangerous, and because they could get away with it.

"Now, if I'd been a little *paler*," he said, and he tipped back his head and laughed, like it was a joke on both of us. If I could talk to him now, I'd tell him that wasn't the only way of being screwed on the deal. I'd tell him there were other kinds of unfair.

I do my second delivery all the way over to the Elks Club, and then I get a call from Sonny Philips on the CB and have to head back down the River Road to Primus Blake's. I guess the old bird scared up enough money to fill his oil tank. At least I'll end up near the lot, I think.

The road runs close to the river, then drifts away.

I watch the woods and think about Hitchcock. He was one of the biggest names in the state for a while, and I got some ink of my own just by fighting him tough. He was a real fighter, hit me harder than anybody in D'Amico's camp ever did; had a way of throwing a hook that started out low and came up over your guard that I never figured out. I remember how he had me on the ropes when the bell rang to end our first fight, how hard it was to stand steady while we waited for the referee to make the call. I remember thinking that maybe I'd won and just didn't know it, and it makes me blush to think how surprised I was when it was Hitchcock's hand that got raised. I guess I wasn't thinking straight.

I remember Terry tapping me on the arm and saying, "Good fight, kid."

I'd run into him in Portland afterwards, and he'd always stop and say hello, even when he was flying high. He respected me, and later on, when a payday was going to fall through for him, I was the guy he had Silverman bring in. I fought him hard again that time. He knocked me out, but it took him eleven rounds, and things were pretty tight on the cards when it happened. I busted one of his ribs, it turned out. It was probably my best effort ever.

I got some decent fights after that, enough to put some cash away. And I kept on fighting longer than I probably should have, just because I didn't know what else to do with myself. Finally, though, I took on this farm kid from Aroostook County, and he not only went the distance with me, but broke my nose for good measure, and after that I was smart enough to call it a day. I wasn't going to end up like Ali, all shaky and pathetic, or dead, like The Pink Cat. I had that money in the bank, and I was going to maybe go back to school and learn a trade.

While I'm at Primus's filling the tank, this guy is shooting baskets at the hoop over the barn door. I'm surprised he can see well enough in the twilight, but he fires away, taking these old-fashioned set shots. After one the ball hits a rock and bounces over my way, and I stop it with my foot and kick it back. When the guy picks it up he squints at me, then comes closer and points.

"Arnold Stimpson!" he says.

He walks up with the ball under his arm, sticks out his other hand, and says, "Eric Lunden; remember me? How long you been back in town?"

"Not that long."

I do remember him, then, running around town, eight or ten years older. I'm surprised he recognizes me, since he left when I was still pretty small, but then he tells me it's because he was living in Portland and saw me fight Terry Hitchcock at the Expo.

"Ouch," I say.

"No, you took it to him," Eric says. "He got lucky."

"That's one way to look at it."

"I remembered you when I read the write-ups," he says, and I wait for him to bring up my little childhood indiscretion. It was in every article, pretty much—how I came out of the State Farm, and why I was there—but before he can, I'm saved by the bell. The fuel gun clanks and jerks off, and I get busy yanking the gun out and sticking it into its cradle on the truck, shutting the PTO off, letting the pressure hiss away.

He waits, smiling, bouncing the ball, alternating hands.

I put a foot up on the running board and the receipt book on my knee and write out the slip. Then I tear off Primus's copy and hand it to him.

"Mind seeing he gets this?"

"Sure, I'll see him at supper, if he lives that long."

I laugh and say it was good to bump into him. I grab the steering wheel, pull myself up into the truck.

Eric says something about getting together for a beer, then waves and heads back to the basket, dribbling the ball behind his back, stopping and popping from fifteen feet out. I wait until the shot swishes through, beep the horn, turn the key, and drive out onto the River Road.

A week later I'm sitting at the table in the old brooder coop, digging into a plate of SpaghettiOs, when the phone rings. I pick it up and hear: "How's it going, brother?"

"Terry?" I say. "How'd you get this number?"

"Silverman gave it to me."

"I didn't know he had it."

"He did. So listen, did you think it over?"

"I didn't have to."

"Did you think about the money?"

"Mainly I thought that comebacks are for suckers."

"Not this one," he says. "Listen, we'll call it Hitchcock–Stimpson Three! Equal billing, my brother!" He goes on, describing the publicity he'll arrange, blowing smoke about how tough I was, and how he wants a good opponent to start with so they'll take him seriously again, and I let him keep talking. It's nice to just listen. I've been sitting alone in the coop, drinking Narragansett from the old lady's stash in the fridge, eating canned food, and maybe I'm a little lonely.

Then he says something about taking it easy on me, and I feel the old temper kick in.

"Nobody ever had to carry Arnold Stimpson."

He laughs. "That's my boy."

I hang up then, and when he calls right back I let it ring.

When it finally stops, the food's cold and I'm not hungry anymore anyway. I scrape my plate and wash the dishes and towel them dry. Then I put on my jacket and go outside. It's dark and cold, and I look up the hill at the crab-apple grove and my grandfather's old house. Somebody I don't know lives there now. After he died they sold the house and the old lady split the money with my uncle Mike, then drank her share all up and had her stroke.

Nice job, Ma.

I walk up the hill to the road. They paved it a few years back, and there are more houses than when I was a kid; there are lights all the way up to the crossing. I walk up that way, looking at my uncle and aunt's house, thinking back, shaking my head. I wonder what

Mark is up to these days. Julie and the rest of them, too. I walk all the way up to the crossing and my ears and face are getting cold, so I turn around and go back and sit in the coop and crack another beer and think about stuff.

❧

So I guess it was a combination of things: staying in the frigging coop again; visiting the old lady and the hostility in her eyes; Silverman and Hitchcock badgering me. And last, but definitely not least, being stupid enough to ask Tomi Lambert if she wanted to go out.

Oh yeah, I asked her.

If you're clueless enough, you can talk yourself into almost anything.

I kept going up to the Neutral Corner when she was working, and I sat at the Mysterious Billy booth because it was near the kitchen, in case she might want to get off her feet again. One evening she was complaining about how tired she was, and I put my fork down and told her I'd like to take her out for a drink after she got off work so she could relax for a change.

She looked surprised. Then she said, "Oh, Arnold," with a look so full of pity that it left me no choice but to find something stupid or reckless to do as soon as humanly possible. I mean, go ahead and tell me I'm an idiot. Tell me I'm ugly or delusional or punch-drunk or just plain full of shit. Tell me you don't go out with former juvenile delinquents.

Just don't look at me like I'm a sad little boy who needs a hug.

I held up a hand while she was still apologizing and said, "Hey, no sweat, it was just a thought," and jumped up like I had a crucial appointment I'd forgotten until that very moment. And when Tomi stood up too and looked into my eyes with that same god-awful tenderness, I grinned like a maniac and snapped off a salute to old Mysterious Billy, went over and paid my bill, and left a tip I couldn't afford. Then I raced home to the coop and dug through the trash until I found Silverman's card.

Some kid sticks his head into the room and says, "You're on," and I feel my stomach roll over. I look at Silverman and he holds up a fist. Same old crap, right down to a sudden attack of cold feet. I spend a few seconds fantasizing about faking an injury, hold it in my mind like a consolation prize. But when Sam says, "Let's do it, champ," I put on my robe and follow him down a corridor into the arena. It's noisy inside, nearly a full house.

Somebody boos when we start down the aisle.

I trail Silverman up to the ring, rolling my shoulders, banging my gloves together, seating them around my knuckles. My hands are taped and sweaty inside the gloves, and I'm loose from shadowboxing.

The ring is smoky under the hanging lights.

Silverman spreads the ropes and I duck through and bounce into my corner and shake out my arms. I grab the ropes and do a couple of knee bends as I look around at the crowd.

I grin, like my mouth isn't as dry as the Sahara of Maine.

When I turn back, Hitchcock is snapping his head like there's water in his ears. He looks about four feet wide, and I feel a little panic start up. But I tamp it down and manage to sneer.

The ref motions to us and we meet in the middle of the ring.

I look at a pimple on Terry's forehead, imagine jabbing it. He's carrying a few extra pounds and his skin is shiny, and the ref is already sweating through his striped jersey. He instructs us about illegal stuff, tells us to fight clean but protect ourselves at all times.

Hitchcock sticks his gloves out, I tap them with my own, and he gives me this grin as if to say, *Here we go again, brother!*

I shuffle to my corner and grab the ropes. I do a deep knee bend, look out at the crowd. I don't see Eric Lunden or anyone else I know, even though Alva Potter put a fight poster in the window a week in advance. I guess it wasn't exciting enough to drag anybody all the way to Portland.

Then I see the two swanks, just showing up. I guess they're real fans, after all. They move along the row, saying, *Sorry, sorry,* and finally reach their seats. The guy holds up a hand and the girl slaps him five. They settle themselves and look toward me, and just for a second, looking back into that killer girl's eyes, I forget where I am or what the hell I'm supposed to be doing.

I guess that's why they call them knockouts, right?

But then Sam says, "Thirty seconds!" and I have to get myself squared away.

Because, of course, I haven't actually gone anywhere. Nope, I'm still right here in the ring. And Terry Hitchcock is still snorting and pawing on the other side. And any second now that bell will clang, and I'll have to come out fighting.

Susan

Tomi calls at four thirty to say she has to work late again because another girl has gone home sick. She won't be getting out until God knows when.

"I hate to ask," she says, "but could you possibly keep the girls overnight?"

"Of course," Susan says. "But I don't know why it's always you."

"I don't know either."

"You should have a talk with Alva."

"Maybe," Tomi laughs, "but now would *not* be the time."

"Do tell."

"He's all worked up over Johnny Lunden. Johnny came in for a drink and nobody noticed how bad he was until he fell off the barstool. You know how he covers it up sometimes. So anyway, the bartender shut him off and he made a huge ruckus. Alva tried to talk to him, so Johnny shoved him and pushed a table over and ran outside. I guess he went berserk in the street. Chief Foss had to haul him off, kicking and screaming."

"Oh, no. Poor Johnny."

"I know," Tomi says.

"He's such a lost soul."

"Well, Chief Foss found him. Mom, I have to go. His Highness is staring."

"All right. Don't worry about the girls."

"You're a peach."

Susan hangs up the phone and turns to look at Olivia and Eloise, who are sitting at the kitchen table, eating molasses cookies and drinking milk from little blue glasses she bought at the five-and-dime.

"That was your mommy," she says.

"Is she coming to get us?" Olivia, the older girl, says.

"She has to work late, so I get to keep you here all night."

"That's okay," Olivia says matter-of-factly.

"That's okay," Eloise says, in an almost perfect imitation, eyes on her sister.

Susan smiles. They're such little sweeties. She hopes it takes a good long while before they get complicated. She knows it will happen eventually; it always does. Girls can be a real handful, she thinks. Tomi certainly was! And she shouldn't talk. She was quite a live wire herself back in the Mesozoic era.

She looks out the window at a fair-weather sky.

At least Tomi's timing is good. Roger has taken Junior out flying, which is just perfect. He loves the girls—but only in small doses. He and Junior will be training all afternoon, then making a night flight to Augusta, which means that when Roger gets home, the girls will already be in bed and he won't have to do anything more than kiss them good night.

Even Roger can handle that much sentiment.

Susan smiles crookedly, sits down with the girls, and helps herself to a cookie.

❧

It's that moment between twilight and nightfall, when the sky is just about to lose its last bit of luminescence. Susan stands hip-shot on the porch, holding her cigarette the way Lauren Bacall used to in the movies: between two fingers, wrist elegantly bent, elbow supported by the other hand.

She takes a puff, tosses her head back to exhale the smoke upward and to the side. This is the way she smoked when she first started, and it's such a flagrant affectation that it makes her laugh to do it now. But she's been thinking about poor Johnny Lunden—he taught her to smoke—and it's taken her back. She can still feel exactly what it was like to be seventeen. She'd wanted so much to be a modern girl, and smoking, of course, gave her a wonderful leg up.

She nips at the cigarette again, listens to the girls playing inside.

My plan has worked to perfection, she thinks, and dramatically exhales another stream of smoke, as if she's said it out loud to Humphrey Bogart. Then she rests her chin on her shoulder and blinks in a sultry way.

"Oh, Lord." She laughs again.

Still holding herself like Bacall, she leans slightly backwards and looks over her shoulder through the window to check on the girls. After feeding them grilled cheese sandwiches and taking them for a walk down the path through the gate to the darkening river (they scared a beaver, and when its tail slapped the water the girls shrieked in mock terror), she herded them back into the house, gave them a ball of yarn, and told them to roll it across the floor for Ginger to chase. They've been happily occupied with that little game for the past fifteen minutes, which has given Susan just enough time to slip out onto the porch and indulge herself.

She takes another peek inside the house.

The cat is rolling herself up into a tangle, kicking and biting at the yarn, and the girls are laughing with a hoarse, clenched ferocity that means they've probably had just about enough.

Susan takes one last drag, walks down the plank steps—imaginary cameras still rolling—and drops the cigarette onto the grass. She puts it out with the toe of her shoe, and nudges it out of sight under the porch.

Then she crosses her arms and looks around at the fields and trees.

It's pretty here, and she loves having a big garden; she loves the field that leads down to their little piece of the river. It's always been nice to be able to shoo your children—or grandchildren—outside without worrying about traffic or strangers or any of that.

Sometimes though, there's a part of her that still wants to be a town girl. It's thinking about her childhood that brings it on, she supposes. It always makes her think of her home—the home she loved so much.

She holds her arms out wide, turns toward the house, dances up the steps to the porch. Inside, she gathers up the yarn and lets the cat out. Then, she takes the girls into the bathroom so they can brush their teeth and wash their faces and hands. She lets them do most of it themselves, before taking control of the washcloth for the finishing touches.

She has their pajamas in the closet, and before long they're in the guest room, tucked in, waiting for their mandatory story. And because Susan has been thinking about being a girl and about the house she grew up in and about Johnny Lunden, she sits on the edge of the bed and says, "Once upon a time, there was a little girl who looked just like Olivia Hurd . . ."

"Like *Eloise* Hurd," the younger girl mumbles sleepily but adamantly.

"Like Olivia *and* Eloise Hurd," Susan says. "And one day this little girl moved to Baxter from a little brick house a long way away . . ."

Susan can clearly remember the ride down from Bangor. It was a warm spring day, much like today. She remembers sitting in the backseat and listening to her parents talk in the front. She remembers crossing the river and looking at the railroad trestle a little downstream, and entering the town, and how different—cozier and prettier—from Bangor it seemed.

They'd parked in front of the hardware store and her father had pulled the directions out of his shirt pocket and checked them. Then he'd gotten out to look at the numbers on the buildings. He came back to say to her mother, "We can walk it from here," with a boyish, expectant grin.

And Susan remembers how they'd proceeded along the street past one beautiful old sea captain's house after another, and how she'd wondered with burgeoning excitement which one it would finally be.

When her father stopped and put his hands on his hips, Susan had held her breath and prayed that he wouldn't shake his head, say, "Nope," and start off again, as he'd done a couple of times along the way. Because this house looked like a fairy-tale castle: tall and white, gabled and filigreed, flanked by high-arching elms.

"This is the one," he'd said then, and they went reverently up to the porticoed front door. Her father knocked and the real estate agent let them in, shaking her father's hand and then her mother's and then Susan's, very gently.

"Welcome to Baxter!" he said. "I think you're going to like it here!"

They followed him through empty, echoy chambers with gleaming hardwood floors—it was much roomier than their house in Bangor—and Susan remembers the narrow passageways that led into mysterious turrets on both sides of the living room. But she wasn't allowed to explore the turrets just yet.

She had followed the grown-ups through another room and up a stairway, and when they got to the top, her father had pointed and said, "This could be your bedroom, honey," and the realtor, hearing this, led them into the wonderful, sunny room with a bay window, an enormous closet, and an expansive, lofty ceiling.

Susan had wanted to stay right there forever.

But the realtor had more to show them.

"See what you think of this!" he'd said, taking them to *another* stairway that led to the attic. He had then conducted them up a short set of steps and through a hatch to an open widow's walk on the roof, where Susan leaned against a wooden railing—her mother's arm around her—and looked all the way across the leafy town to the river.

If they hadn't bought the house after that, Susan would have died. But she'd known better than to plead, because her father had instructed them on the drive down not to appear too eager, even if the place seemed too good to be true.

"They'll jack up the price," he'd said. "Believe me, I've seen it happen."

And they had believed him, of course, because he was a real estate attorney himself, which is how he'd gotten word on the house in the first place, before it even made it onto the market. He'd been looking to move out of Bangor, to find a little town with an abundance of nice old homes and a shortage of legal specialists, and one of his pals in the business had tipped him off about Baxter.

From the widow's walk the real estate agent had pointed out the homes of several of Baxter's leading citizens. He'd given them a little rundown of the town's shipbuilding history, the industry that had made all the big homes possible.

Then he took them back downstairs, and Susan's father had allowed her to run into one of the turrets—they were just round rooms, it turned out—and then to go outside and play, as long as she stayed in the yard, while he and Susan's mother talked with the realtor in the kitchen.

Susan remembers walking out the side door and moseying around the house, trailing a hand along its brick foundation, to the backyard, where she was stunned to see a dirty-faced, towheaded boy in patched overalls hunkered down in the shaggy grass, out of sight of the house behind a prim little shed, fiddling with bits of wood and a cigarette lighter.

She was upset at first to find a strange boy, not only making himself at home on *their* new property, but playing with fire to boot. But since he seemed to be totally unaffected by her arrival, she didn't yell for her parents, and when she walked closer and he finally did look up from his little campfire, it was with such a welcoming, mischievous grin that all she could think to do was crouch down next to him.

"This is my secret hideout," he'd told her. "But you can stay."

"Okay," Susan said.

"Want to help?"

At his direction she peeled wispy bits of birch bark from the orderly row of trees bordering their back lawn, and added twigs and broken pieces of pine shingles from a small assortment beside the cellar door.

They slowly fed the fire, careful it didn't get out of control, too engrossed to talk much more beyond exchanging names and ages. (He was seven, too.) But by the time Susan's father had come outside and called her name, they were well on their way to becoming fast friends.

Her father called her name again, loudly.

Susan yelled, "Coming!," and they'd stomped the flames out and run around to the portico, where the realtor was shaking everyone's hand again and climbing contentedly into his convertible.

"It's been a pleasure doing business with you!" he called over.

Everybody waved as he drove off, and then Mr. O'Leary turned around, put an arm around Susan's mother, and said, "Well, how about that!"

Then he seemed to notice the boy standing beside his daughter for the first time, and he scooched down low to shake the boy's slender hand, asking his name and where he lived.

"Johnny," the boy had said, pointing diagonally across the street to a house that, while not grandly built like the ones on their side of the street, had no doubt once been a perfectly acceptable Cape Cod.

Now, though, it was so obviously neglected—peeling paint, broken porch railings, a cracked window, missing roof shingles—that when the boy asked if it would be all right for Susan to come over and play, her father, having already taken note of his personal dinginess, suggested that for now, he'd prefer they stay right here where he could keep an eye on them. But he winked and said it playfully, so as not to embarrass the boy. Her father was always thoughtful that way.

"And as time went on," Susan says, "the girl and the boy became best friends, and they stayed friends all the way through school." She's still sitting on the edge of the bed, looking at the dark window, speaking in a low voice.

When she stops talking she can hear Eloise breathing deeply, and she would have thought Olivia was asleep, too, but when she leans over to kiss them good night, Olivia's eyes open a fraction.

"I like that boy—that Johnny," Olivia says.

"I like him, too," Susan says. "He was a nice boy."

"What happened to him?"

"Oh, he grew up," Susan says, "just like we all do."

"Not me," Olivia whispers, and then, just like that, she's out.

Susan laughs soundlessly, kisses Olivia's cheek, then walks around to the other side of the bed and kisses Eloise's. She pulls the covers up under their little chins.

Susan is back on the porch, smoking another cigarette, when Roger finally makes it home. He shuts his headlights off, and for a moment she can't see anything. Then it's a clear night again and there are thousands of stars overhead, some bright as anything, others barely visible against the blackness.

Roger limps over from the car. "Is that you, Susan?"

"I suppose it is," Susan says.

"You know how I feel about smoking."

"Why, hello, darling," Susan says. "I missed you too."

Roger stops halfway up the steps and looks at her. The porch light isn't on, and it's dark with just the starlight and a fingernail of a moon over the trees, and she's barely visible. She looks different—something about her posture. He watches the ember at the end of her cigarette rise and brighten, then lower again.

"Is everything all right?" Roger says.

"Oh, of course it is."

Roger watches the ember rise again, then drift off to the side and hold steady. In the vague light, he thinks that Susan has tipped her head to one side. She might be looking at him. He's not sure. Then he hears her long, slow exhalation, and for a moment the smoke lingers between them in the dark country air.

Eric

Eric Lunden is sitting on the baggage belt with James Blake, waiting for the next flight to arrive.

The belt is a relic that Roger Lambert picked up for a song when he transformed Baxter Municipal into Knox County Regional a while back. It's a sort of conveyor with swiveling plates that hooks through the baggage room and disappears under a SAIL THE MID-COAST poster. Eric and James are sipping coffee from Styrofoam cups, keeping an eye out that some wise guy doesn't sneak in and hit the on button that sends the belt lurching into motion. Those twisty plates can do some damage.

They're discussing the new girl Lambert's got working the Avis desk when an elderly dude comes ambling up with his two-wheeler, which means the Maine Air flight is going to land shortly—their cue to get outside.

They ease to their feet and head for the doors, two rangy young guys almost exactly the same size.

Eric says, "Hey, Tate," to the skycap, and the old-timer says, "Eric" right back, with a friendly-enough nod. Then he turns to James and says, "Brother," and they bump knuckles.

Eric and James shove through the double doors, cross to the taxi stand, and drape themselves against James's front fender. It will take a few minutes for the plane to actually land and for the passengers to claim their bags off the old conveyer and come outside.

Eric doesn't mind dawdling there. He and James have become amigos all over again, twenty years later, and it's nice, standing there in shirtsleeves in the sunlight that comes at a slant across the river and settles itself over the airport like a softly shaken blanket. The edge of that blanket flips little dust devils up that kick past them and twirl away along the terminal lane.

After a while Eric looks at James and says, "About all that brother stuff."

"What took you so long?" James says.

"I had to think about it."

James snorts. They often snort at each other.

"No, really," Eric says. "Am I not a cabbie?"

"You are," James drawls.

"Was I not a skycap, too?"

"Rumor has it," James says. He looks into his coffee cup, takes a quick sip.

"If you prick me, do I not bleed?" Eric says.

James rolls his eyes because he knows Eric is showing off. He's way more educated than Eric—has a master's in comparative lit from Columbia, and taught for a while at Quinnipiac. But he also turned out to be someone who couldn't hack academia for whatever reason, which is why he's back in town, temporarily driving taxi for Norm Lavin.

"And where do I abide?" Eric says.

James doesn't bother to answer.

The fact is, Eric has been staying with James at the rooming house. How Eric ended up there was, he came back to Maine to see his mother and brother, and when that went better than expected, he decided to go crazy and look up the old man, too. But Johnny Lunden was at the Togus VA facility, drying out, which meant Eric had to hole up somewhere if he was going to wait, which he decided to do because it had taken him almost a decade to come back this time, and who knew when he'd work up the ambition to try it again.

He ran out of money after a couple of weeks, and Early helped get him in at the airport. He lugged baggage, then jumped to a cabbie job. When James reappeared it was a surprise, but they reconnected easily enough over a few games of horse, and then James began driving too, and they were together a lot, just like the old days.

"That's all well and good," James says now.

"But . . . ?" Eric says archly.

"There's context involved."

"Such as?"

"Well," James says, "one's heritage."

"As to that," Eric says, "who can ever really say?"

And he puts an arm next to James's. He's a bit olive-y anyway, and likes his sun, and James isn't a hell of a lot darker, truth be told. Eric shakes his arm to emphasize the scant difference.

"Are you making some kind of a point?" James says.

"A family of Nordics," Eric says, "and I show up."

"So there was an Italian in the woodpile."

Eric laughs.

The terminal doors bump open then, but it's only Lambert's kid hustling off on some errand.

Eric looks back at James. "So listen, one day in Portland I closed the bar at this hotel, okay? And while I was walking across the parking lot, these two assholes came out of one of those street-level rooms, yelling the N-word."

James raises his eyebrows. "At you?"

"I shit you not."

"Huh," James says. "Continue."

"When they got close one of them said, 'Hey, you ain't a—!' " Eric makes a nasty face to indicate the unspoken word. "Then they turned around," he says, "and went back from whence they came."

"Crestfallen, no doubt," James says.

"Crushed," Eric says.

"Poor lads," James says. "Racists have feelings too, you know."

"Anyway, the point is—"

"The point is, it was dark out and they were probably drunk."

They work on their coffee. Pretty soon the Maine Air twin lands and rolls out and taxis toward the terminal. It's the only scheduled carrier that comes into Baxter, a little commuter that flies Cessnas back and forth to Boston.

"Another time," Eric says, and James groans.

"No, listen. I'm walking back from the store with a six-pack, and this girl I happen to know is going the other way, and it seems like she's purposefully not looking at me, so when we're about to pass I reach out and grab her arm. She jumps a foot. 'Oh, my God!' she says. 'I thought you were some black dude.' "

"Well!" James says. "No wonder she jumped."

"She didn't mean it like that. Anyway, the point is—"

"Yeah, I know." James finishes his coffee and takes the empty cup across to the trash can next to the terminal doors. There's a paperback sticking out of his back pocket. He and Eric are both notorious for reading in the cabs—it drives Lavin crazy—but James's books are apt to have the word *treatise* on their covers, while Eric's tend more toward busty blondes and revolvers.

James comes back and the old baggage belt starts up—you can hear it lurching and clanking into gear—and Eric warns, "I got more," as he drifts down to his own cab to wait.

"I'm sure you do," James says.

After ten minutes the clatter shuts down and people start coming outside. First are a couple of old ladies, arms linked, dragging suitcases on wheels. Seeing James in the number-one spot, they veer toward Eric, smiling like harpies.

"Sorry, ladies," Eric says. "That other gentleman is first."

James snorts under his breath. One of the old ladies rolls her eyes over toward him and then back to Eric, staring fixedly, trying to will him into some kind of tribal understanding.

"No problem, ladies," James calls over. "It's perfectly all right."

"Absolutely not!" Eric protests. "I wouldn't think of it!"

It's all bullshit, of course. James is pretending to be unflappable, and Eric is feigning righteousness, but actually neither wants anything to do with the old ladies because whoever transports them will inevitably have to hump their bags up three flights of stairs into a place that smells like stale crumpets and old cat litter in exchange for a minuscule tip, if any. Eric has the leverage, though, because James *is* first up, so when he marches them over and more or less stuffs them into James's cab, James can't do anything about it.

"There you go, brother," Eric says.

James smirks. He walks around the front of the car and gets in behind the wheel. He looks over his shoulder and says, "To the Ritz, ladies?"

"What?" one of the old ladies honks. "No!"

James puts the cab in gear and pulls out into the lane. He leans sideways and throws the meter as they head off. Eric gets into his own cab and moves it up to the first position. When two suits come out of the terminal, heading his way, he scrambles to get the door for them. They walk right past, though—they've got somebody waiting in the temporary lot—without even an apologetic glance.

Eric throws the door shut a little harder than necessary.

"Excuse me?" someone says then.

This skinny kid is dragging a big case on wheels with one hand and holding a duffel over his shoulder with the other.

Eric looks around, hoping one of the Vietnamese cabbies might be pulling in. They're usually happy to take anybody at all. If Eric was to walk down and say, "You want this kid?," either one would jump at the chance and maybe even thank him in the process. But they're not around, so it looks like the joke might be on Eric. James will have a good laugh when he hears who Eric ended up with.

Or *with whom I ended up*, Eric will have to say, or James will correct him.

"Excuse me, sir?" the kid says again.

Eric looks a little more carefully at him. Blond hair, nice teeth. Sometimes you can't tell because they all dress alike—this kid has cutoff jeans and a Red Sox T-shirt—but then you hear them speak and revise your original estimation.

"Okay," he says. He pops the trunk and wrestles the big case in. "Oof!"

The kid laughs. "Sorry."

"That makes two of us," Eric says. "What the heck are you smuggling?"

"Just my cello."

Eric's mental cash register dings again.

He puts the other bag in and goes for the door. The kid asks if he can ride in front, and that's usually a no-no, but Eric doubts this kid is going to be much of a threat. This little rich kid home from music camp. He projects a big tip for delivering the family scion home safely.

His imagination takes over then, and he pictures Mommy, the nubile trophy wife, coming out to pay in her bathrobe, fresh from a steamy shower, all pink and moist and probably halfway to a self-induced climax because her aging and fabulously wealthy husband has run off to the hedge fund office with barely a backwards glance.

Eric throws the meter. "Camden?" he says. "Chestnut Street, perhaps?"

The kid looks at him. "How'd you know?"

"Can't tell," Eric says happily. "Trade secret."

They pull into the terminal lane and roll out to the River Road. Eric drives up to Baxter and along the Speedway to Route 1. He stops at the intersection across from the Elks Club building, and while they're waiting, remembers asking James if he wanted to go over for a swim after work, and the way James looked at him, as if he had two heads.

"The *Elks* Club?" James said. "Serious?"

It took Eric a moment. "You can't swim there?"

"Is there a Sons of the Confederacy nearby?" James said. "Maybe we could drop in for lunch afterwards."

Eric apologized, but James threw him to the wolves anyway by telling Lavin about the invitation.

Lavin barked out a laugh around his soggy, unlit cigar.

"Can I go too?" he rasped. "Hey, go get Trang and his old man—we'll invade the sonofabitches!"

It makes Eric cringe now to look at the place. But then there's a break in traffic and he whips the cab out onto Route 1 and heads for Camden.

About halfway there, the kid says, "How *did* you guess Chestnut Street, anyway?"

"It was the cello," Eric says.

The kid smiles and looks out the window. They pass the new McDonald's and run along past the hospital and through Rockport and on to Camden. They go into town to the five-way intersection and double back onto Chestnut Street.

Riding up the hill, Eric looks out at the harbor and all the jutting masts. A block further and they're smack-dab in the high-rent district, impressive old homes rising on both sides of the elm-lined street.

"Tell me when," Eric says.

"Right there," the kid says, pointing at a tall Victorian with a colonnaded porch, huge bay windows, fancy scroll-worked eaves, and a wide lawn stretching downhill toward the water.

The gate is open so Eric drives on in. He takes them to the top of the drive and the kid says, "Keep going," pointing to an offshoot that leads around the corner of the house.

"What, the servants' entrance?"

"Pretty much," the kid says. He shrugs and smiles.

They follow the drive to a smaller place, built in the same style as the big house. Probably the carriage house originally, and Eric gets why the kid thinks it's funny.

"Home, sweet home," the kid says.

Eric helps him in with his stuff, and isn't surprised when his mother turns out to be your plain, ordinary mom in her thirties, tired-looking, a little rushed. She's nice enough, though, and gives Eric a decent gratuity.

You never can tell.

Eric walks outside and the kid follows.

"My mom *works* for the rich folks," he says. "That's who paid for music camp. Braces, too," he adds, showing his teeth. He watches Eric get in the cab and waves, sort of clumsily, the way kids do.

Eric waves back and drives down Chestnut.

He doubles back through town, thinking about the kid and his mom. Then he uses the rest of the ride to rehearse a story for James, the one he was getting ready to tell when the Maine Air flight came in. He wants to get the details right.

It's a good story that starts with him quitting his family and escaping to Florida, but he thinks maybe he'll skip that part and go right to when he ran out of money and got caught stealing food. From there on it's *really* good—how they took him into a back room at the grocery store and sat him down next to another kid they'd busted. How his ill-gotten steak and the other kid's pilfered ham sat on the table, tagged as evidence, and how the other kid grinned at him and said, "Nice timing, brother."

"Shut up, you two," the man guarding them said. He was watching through a window for other scofflaws. He hadn't spotted any by the time the cops came and took Eric and his new acquaintance outside.

The other kid's name was Jerrod, and they talked all the way to the hoosegow.

After Eric explained about Portland, Jerrod said, "You came all the way down here to get busted?"

"Expanding my horizons," Eric said.

Jerrod laughed. They rode on, trying to stay upright on the bouncing bench seats. It wasn't easy because they'd been left handcuffed. Finally they arrived and their driver marched them inside and they were booked: fingerprints, shoelaces and belts, wallets, the whole deal.

"What's this?" Jerrod said. "Crime of the century?"

"Shut your mouth," the cop inking his thumb said.

When they were grudgingly offered a phone call, Jerrod shook his head, but Eric called Maine and left a message with Mr. Realtor—his stepfather—just on the odd chance that he'd actually pass it on to Eric's mother.

It was getting dark when they reached a big communal cell with bunks at one end and showers at the other, and eight other occupants. The door clanged shut with a sound just like in the movies, and the sheriff shuffled off without a backward glance.

Eric tried not to seem too nervous, but stuck pretty close to his new friend, who seemed to know people from the way he was reaching out, tapping fingers, mumbling greetings.

"Who's your friend, Jerrod?"

The speaker was sitting on a cot under the single barred window. He was probably forty, and had a definite air of authority. He looked sort of fierce, actually.

"Caught us the same place, X," Jerrod said.

The older man stood up and looked into Eric's eyes. They were the same height, but he outweighed Eric by forty pounds or so.

"What's a skinny little boy like you doing in jail?" he said.

"I don't know," Eric said. "I was trying to steal something to eat."

"Trying to steal you some supper!" He looked around the cell. "I guess we got us a hard case here!" Everybody laughed, and he looked back at Eric. "What's your name, son?"

"Eric." It seemed like a silly name, compared to X.

Eric felt awkward, standing there while the other man gave him the once-over, wondering whether he was supposed to say something more. But then the other man nodded.

"All right," he said. "You heard him call me X?"

"Yes, sir," Eric said.

"That's because I rejected the white man's slave name."

"Don't blame you," Eric said, ludicrously.

X stared a little harder, but let it go. He held a hand upright, and after Eric figured out what was expected, they shook, brother-style. Then X nodded and said, "You can call me X, too, since you in here with the rest of us."

"I think I'll just go with 'sir.' "

X grinned at Jerrod. "Your friend's all right."

Then he looked back at Eric. "All right, come on and join us. Come on, y'all," he said, turning to include everybody else. "Fall in."

They lined up and he led them in small-space calisthenics, talking the whole time, exhorting them to work hard, to stay strong. They went at it long enough that when X called a stop, Eric was exhausted. He was proud he'd made it through, though.

Everybody headed for the showers, so he fell in and took his turn. There were two stations with four showerheads each, and they stood in two circles, sneaking looks at one another as the water hissed down. There was a pile of rough towels, and they dried off and put their clothes back on.

Eric stretched out on the cot next to Jerrod's and lay quietly. Voices rumbled, the men conversing in twos and threes. Eric could hear yelling and swearing from other cells, some of it in Spanish. Then the lights went low and it got relatively quiet, but you could still hear doors opening and shutting, people calling out. At one point something rang like a school bell, then there was a loud, extended buzz.

Eric wouldn't have thought he'd be able to sleep, but sometime later, when he heard his name called, then called loudly again, he realized he'd been lost to the world. He sat up, remembering where he was. There was a beefy guard hulking outside the cell door.

"I said get on out here," he said.

There are two empty cabs at the taxi stand, Trang's and James's. Nobody's in the baggage area, so Eric goes into the little coffee shop and gets a cup to go. Trang's sitting at the counter, and he smiles and says hello.

Eric walks down to the new end of the terminal and finds James by the door opposite the ticket counter, talking to Early and Tate, both old-timers sitting in plastic chairs against the wall. James is waving his arms and stalking around tight-assed, and the two older men are leaning against each other, lifting their feet up and down, helpless expressions on their faces.

When Eric walks up, James turns with leftover tears in his eyes.

"What's so funny?" Eric says.

"Oh, nothing much."

The old-timers giggle, and James rolls his eyes. "Foolish old men. Let's get outside."

"Gentlemen," Eric says to the skycaps. He turns to follow James.

"So long, brother," Tate croaks behind him.

"Hush, now," Early Blake says.

James looks back at them but doesn't say anything. Eric catches up and they walk to the baggage area, pass through the double doors, and cross the lane to the taxi stand.

Trang is standing at attention by his cab, first up, and he waves and smiles. Eric waves back and leans against James's vehicle, turning his face up to the sun. It's still nice, with just enough breeze to keep things comfortable. He waits like that until James clears his throat and says, "Well, let's hear the rest of it."

But Eric just says, "That's all right," because he's changed his mind about Florida. It's not just that business in the terminal, either. He was already having second thoughts, because in reviewing the story, in taking it all the way to the end, he'd remembered a couple of things. Like how after letting him out of the cell, the guard matter-of-factly locked the rest of them back in, as if that was a normal thing to do. And how when Eric said, "Take it easy, you guys," nobody in the cell acknowledged him—not X, not even Jerrod.

"Suit yourself," James says. And the *brother* that he might have added lolls between them, like some kind of ghostly balloon. They're both quite aware of it, but neither says anything. It could be that they're a little self-conscious, at least for the moment. Or maybe it's just gotten too noisy, because inside the terminal the old baggage belt has lurched back to life, and it's not a bit quieter than it ever was. They listen as it rumbles along its same old track, carrying the same old baggage. They picture it, twisting and swiveling through the archaic end of the building, no doubt just dying to pinch somebody's unsuspecting ass.

Johnny and Early

When the day finally arrives, Johnny Lunden is supposed to hang out until the volunteer shows up. And he tries his best to comply.

But the volunteer is taking forever, and Johnny's dying to get away from this old brick compound. It's not that he's not grateful; he's just had enough looking after. They've looked after him with drugs, with therapy and pep talks, and he's had enough. He wants to go home and see if it works. He lasts another hour, pacing around the little room. Then he says, "Balderdash!" and shoves open the window. He horses his sea bag over the sill, works it to the side, and hears it thump to the ground. He folds himself through the window and backs down the fire escape.

Johnny doesn't really have to do it this way.

They've signed off on his paperwork, after all. He could just walk out the front door. But then someone would stop him in the lobby and advise him to wait, and they'd have to discuss it.

"Discussing" is another thing he's had about enough of.

There's a drop at the bottom of the ladder, and when he lands it sends a shock through his bones, which reminds him that he's no spring chicken anymore. He's not sure how that happened. Somebody flipped the calendar a few pages when he wasn't looking.

Anyway, he has to crouch there a moment to get his breath back. Then he shoulders the sea bag and skulks away through the shadows.

James Blake drives the last nail in and walks the length of the dock, using his body weight to test the new boards. Eric Lunden stands on the trampled grass nearby, leaning on a leftover length of planking.

"Dinah will be happy," Eric says.

James looks up the path. "Here they come now."

Early Blake and Dinah come up and stand beside Eric.

"Will wonders never cease!" Dinah says.

Early and James smile at each other.

"It was getting to be more holes than boards!"

"Well, it's all boards now," Early says.

Dinah walks out onto the dock, gives James a hug.

"We should probably try it out," James says over her shoulder.

"You think?" Eric says.

"Absolutely." James lets go of Dinah. "How about you, Grandpa?"

"No, you boys go ahead."

"Ma?"

"You know better than that."

James looks at Eric. "I guess it's just us chickens."

Johnny walks down the long drive to Route 17, studying the cars coming into the facility. Maybe one of them is his volunteer, but it's too late now; he has to keep moving. Things are starting to tighten up a little, and the one thing he's found that usually helps is movement. Aside from his old friend Jack, of course. But he's supposed to be leaving Jack alone. That's sort of the whole point. It's strange to be on the other side of it, though. He feels it hiking, like some of his joints are slung all wrong.

Johnny stops to shrug the sea bag a little higher.

Give it a chance, he thinks. You wanted this. It's a good thing.

He'd always thought that one day he would get fed up and quit, and when they sentenced him to the VA, he figured the time had come. He'd go through the program and get it started, and once he got out he'd find a way to hang on. He imagined it would be prickly but doable.

He was definitely right about the prickly part.

Here's hoping about the rest, Johnny thinks.

He looks at the fat clouds: *You can send those angels anytime.*

This is an old tongue-in-cheek plea, a droll invocation of his childhood prayers, something he's tossed off at odd moments ever since he can remember. He knows exactly when it started—trying to patch up Rifleman Chester C. Williams in the middle of a firefight—but it didn't work then, any more than it worked when he was eight, hiding under the porch with his hands pressed together. So he doesn't quite know why he bothers with it now.

"Can't hurt," he says out loud. And he keeps moving.

"Those boys going fishing?" Primus says from his rocker on the porch. He's sunken into himself a lot the past couple of years, and is starting to look like one of those wizened little apple people they sell at fairs.

"I guess they are, Daddy."

Early looks toward the river, where James and Eric are stepping gingerly into Early's wobbly boat. They've unloaded all the clamming gear—rollers, rakes, boots, and gloves—and left them in a jumble on the dock. Early watches until they're safely seated.

"Never knew you to miss out on a fishing trip," Primus says.

"I've got an errand to run." Early pats the old man on his shoulder, goes inside to tell Dinah he's headed out. She nods toward the river, where James is backing them smokily away from the dock.

"What about young Lunden?"

"We decided to make it a surprise."

"I hope you know what you're doing."

"That makes two of us," Early says.

Johnny's only a mile down 17 when this old pickup towing a hog trailer comes along, and the driver, after squinting at him, pulls over and sticks his hand out the window, twirling it for Johnny to come on.

Johnny rolls his bag into the back, climbs in the front.

Turns out his benefactor is a former Marine who stopped because of the sea bag. When he learns Johnny was a recon medic, he's even friendlier, and as they jounce along he blows billows of pipe smoke and tells Johnny all about the Common Ground Fair and the blue ribbon he should've won if the fix wasn't in, if the judge hadn't decided to give it to his own goddamn son-in-law.

"That sounds about right," Johnny says.

"Don't it?" the farmer says. "What a world we live in."

They swap battle tales for a few miles and then the farmer decides he'll take Johnny all the way to North Union. He'd take him right to his doorstep, he says, except he's got another stop to make and he can't be late.

"You're already doing too much."

"Not for you, Doc," the farmer says.

It bucks Johnny up a little. A Marine calling you "Doc" was always a good thing.

In Union the farmer pulls over onto the shoulder. Johnny grabs his duffel out of the back, leans in to shake hands.

"You take care of yourself," the farmer says. "I mean it."

He pulls a U-turn, and as he drives off the hog inside the trailer grunts resoundingly, like some kind of mythic beast.

Early stops in town to get a cup of coffee for the ride.

Tomi Lambert takes his money and gives him one of her sweet smiles.

"How are those girls of yours?" Early asks.

"They're a handful."

"Just like their mama."

"Stop it." Tomi hands him his change, and when he drops it into the tip cup, smiles again. Early brushes aside a quick yearning, like he's done for thirty-odd years now. Vangie ruined him for anyone else, but that's never stopped the feeling from coming along now and then on its own. He chides himself for a silly old fool and heads for the door, scanning the pictures on the walls. Sometimes Alva Potter will come up with somebody new. But Early doesn't see anything different. Rocky still has his spot by the window, and Ali is still dancing over the bar, glaring down at Sonny Liston.

Johnny walks onto the little bridge and holds the rail. The Baxter is fast up here, a little frantic. He watches it toss and swirl, then hefts the bag and crosses to the other side.

He looks at the long stretch of road ahead and wishes he still had the old Indian. He'd love to be flying along, letting the wind knock the wicked out of him. But he hasn't had that bike for five years, since he wiped out on the flats between Baxter and Rockland. They said he was three sheets to the wind, but that patch of oil would've gotten anyone, and he was sober enough to lay the bike down. It would've been just scrapes and bruises if somebody hadn't put a guardrail in just the wrong place.

As it was he came out of it with a broken leg, a ruptured spleen, a dislocated shoulder, a grade-three concussion, and about an acre of missing skin. Johnny thinks he must have looked like one of his old combat patients, hobbling out of the VA a month later in a walking cast.

Early's favorite route to Togus is to follow the Baxter on country roads as far as he can, and then to go cross-country past Damariscotta Lake and come into the facility from the south. It's a little bit longer, but he hates the traffic on Route 17, which is a two-lane with lots of curves and hills. It's not that he wants to go fast, either; it's just that other vehicles do, and they end up tailgating him.

When Early checks in, the woman at the desk smiles and tells him to have a seat while they go after Corpsman Lunden. He eases into a heavy wooden chair, crosses his legs, and stares at the framed portraits of famous Maine soldiers on the wall across the room. Joshua Chamberlain is the only one he recognizes, because of the walrus mustache. He looks a little like Johnny, now that Early thinks about it.

Early shifts on the hard seat—damn his bony ass—and rehearses what he'll say when they bring Johnny down. Probably nothing about Eric. Johnny's never known how to talk about his kids, and there's no reason to think it'd be any different now. He'll just take him down to the farm for a meal. Then he'll put them together.

But when the same woman comes over a few minutes later, it's to tell him they can't seem to find Corpsman Lunden. She's wondering if there was a mix-up and he got a ride with someone else, and apologizes if that's the case. She'd hate to think he came all this way for nothing.

Johnny has a very hard time walking past the Town Line Market, because he happens to know it houses one of the finest beer coolers in the region. He can almost feel the ice-cold can on his cheek, can almost taste the lovely, bitter, frosty liquid going down his dusty throat.

A dozen rationalizations form in his mind, and it becomes almost impossible to keep moving; it's like getting caught on the flats after the tide has turned, wading through knee-deep water toward shore.

But just as he reaches the store's driveway, an old, two-door Plymouth Valiant comes chattering past, slows with its brake lights on, and pulls over to stop in front of him.

Johnny knows right off it's Early Blake, who's been driving that same push-button rig since Christ was a corporal. He lugs the bag up and looks in the driver's-side window, and it warms his heart to see old Early *almost* smiling back. He's always figured a near smile from Early was worth a horse laugh from anyone else.

"Mr. Blake," Johnny says.

"Mr. Lunden," Early says. "Hop in."

Early's got to be in his mid-seventies, but he looks younger except for his hair, which has gone all white.

Johnny tries to figure how long it's been. Not that it matters; things stay pretty much the same between them. Early's had a soft spot for him since he used to ride his bicycle down the River Road to play with Earl Jr., and Johnny's always felt the same about Early, a man who would let a stray kid hang around for hours on end, and never treat him any different than his own.

Johnny gives the store a last look, works his bag onto the backseat, and squeezes into the front. Early punches buttons, eases out onto the road, and accelerates slowly. He won't be hurried, and five other vehicles whip around the Valiant and race off ahead of them before he finally gets up to speed.

Johnny smiles. It's nice that *some* things never change.

James and Eric ran downriver almost to the Keag and now are slowly making their way back. The breeze changed with the tide and it's a slow, cool, and choppy ride. James is on the rear thwart, hand on the throttle, and Eric is trolling off to the side, keeping the line well out so it won't tangle in the prop. They haven't hit any stripers, but it's late in the season, so that's no surprise. They're mostly out just to give Eric something to do. Fixing the dock was supposed to do the trick, but you couldn't hurry Early, and they were all through with it by the time he finally hit the road.

Eric jerks the rod higher, holds it there a moment.

"Get a nibble?" James says.

"I thought I felt something. Maybe not."

"Sometimes it'll trick you."

Eric lets the rod down again.

The river loops back under the road, and they come up on Ragged Pond and then climb a long, wooded incline. They ride to the top, slow but steady, like the Little Engine That Could.

"That was quite a show you put on uptown," Early says to Johnny Lunden.

"So I heard," Johnny says.

Early huffs a little laugh. "I hope they helped you out at Togus."

"They gave it the old college try," Johnny says.

Early gives him a look.

They ride down the backside of the hill and stop at the Route 90 light. A flatbed hauling a skidder turns in front of them and starts back the way they came, gears grinding and engine growling as it crawls up the grade.

Johnny turns to watch it go over the crest of the hill. He's worked in the woods some, and has always liked skidders, how strange they look, like machines built on another planet.

"Do you still have a place to go?" Early says.

"I should be fine."

Johnny *hopes* his stuff is still in his little apartment, and that his key will still work. He's lived there for years and has always gotten along with the landlord; in fact, they've played cards and drunk together many times, which ought to count for something.

"You're welcome to come down to the farm," Early says.

"Oh, I couldn't do that."

"I don't see why not."

"Dinah would give you hell."

The light changes and Early punches buttons and drives them through the intersection. "She's already signed off on it," he says, and after a moment Johnny knows this means something, but it takes him a little while longer to figure out what.

They pass a pond and one of those old, fenced-in family graveyards. Then Johnny says, "Wait—you were the volunteer?"

"Did you think it was pure luck?"

"I thought it was some kind of a sign."

"It still might be," Early says.

They ride past a greenhouse on Johnny's side. It has young trees with bagged roots leaning against the office and one of those message signs beside the road that always has a different gardening pun.

"POTTING IS SUCH SWEET SORROW!" it says today.

Johnny watches the sign go by. He's still a little confounded.

Early turns onto the Old County Road so they can skip Rockland. They pass farmhouses and a used-car business, a big cemetery and the long, flooded Rockland quarry. Johnny has a quick thought about another quarry, and realizes how shaky he still is when it brings him close to tears.

He shuts his eyes and keeps them that way until they turn right, roll into Baxter, and stop at the light. Then he blinks and looks at Early.

Early looks back with his eyebrows up.

And Johnny tries, he really does. He tries to envision walking into the farmhouse with Early, saying hello to Dinah and ancient old Primus, standing there waiting for whatever came next. But the image won't quite settle into something plausible, and finally he tells Early he probably ought to check out his own place before he does anything else.

"It'll still be here when you get back," Early says.

"I know, but I'm kind of anxious."

The light turns green and Early shoots them over to the hardware store. This is just about at the scene of the crime, Johnny realizes. Not that he remembers it all that well, but he does know where it took place, and he has flashes of reeling into the street to direct traffic; he remembers drunkenly supple bows and flourishes. He doesn't remember why he thought it was necessary, but people were laughing, and that made him angry, and he remembers kicking at car doors, and fighting with somebody who didn't appreciate it, and he thinks it might have ended with him taking a poke at Chief Foss, although the chief didn't mention that when they were trying to decide between jail and Togus.

"How about I wait for you, then," Early says.

And Johnny almost lets it happen. If Early would say one more thing, in fact, he probably would. But Early's gone as far as he can now, asking twice, and eventually Johnny lays his head over and says, "I sure did appreciate the ride, Mr. Blake."

"Go on, then," Early says.

Johnny knows his feelings are hurt. But when he slides out and blows Early a kiss, Early can't help a little smile. That seems to tick him off even more, though, and he doesn't look at Johnny again as he backs away from the curb and drives off, punching buttons.

"Skunked, huh?" old Primus says when James comes up to the porch. He laughs until it turns into a cough that hunches him over.

"Easy there," James says.

"Skunked!" Primus says through the coughing.

Eric comes out of the barn. He's cleaned all the fishing gear and put it away, but still can't hold still. "Got anything else that needs doing?"

"You can split up some firewood." James nods toward the woodpile.

"Sounds good." Eric starts over.

"Don't cut your foot off," James calls after him.

"I'll try not to."

Primus starts coughing again, deep croaks that leave him breathless, and James sits down with his great-grandfather and pats him between the shoulder blades. He has to be exquisitely careful. It feels like he's patting a little bundle of brittle sticks.

Johnny drops the bag on the landing and digs the key out of the flowerpot on the railing. He brushes it clean, tries it in the door, and finds it still works. Thank God for small favors, he thinks, and hauls the bag into the kitchen.

The next thing he does is walk around to the front room and open the window. There's a nice breeze off the river, and he sticks his head out to take a look around. Straight down is the green awning over the hardware store; to the left is the monument—a Union soldier, rifle on shoulder—and farther down the town cemetery.

Past the cemetery, behind a weeping willow, he catches glimpses of the house where he grew up, the white clapboards, the front porch. He's lost track of who lives there now—his own parents sold out while he was in the Pacific; he hasn't seen them since—but they've done a good job fixing it up.

Johnny pulls a chair close to the window. He's always liked to people-watch from here, especially on a Saturday when everybody is in town. It's like being an anthropologist, he thinks, observing the Baxterian in his native habitat. Or an alien, maybe, studying life on Earth.

But that thought brings to mind another house and another family, and he's in no shape to think about them just now.

Johnny looks toward the stoplight, watches the traffic come up.

There's a pickup loaded with rollers and rakes, a convertible with four young people—the driver turning to swat at one of his backseat passengers—and Sonny Philips's oil truck, air brakes wheezing as it decelerates. Then a little red VW joins the queue, and Johnny thinks: Susie O'Leary!

He's seen her riding around in that bug.

The light changes, and the vehicles move slowly into town. Susie is steering with one hand, her other elbow out the window. She was always an easy and elegant driver, the first one of their little gang to have a car, and he remembers riding around with her just like those kids in the convertible.

Opposite his window she looks up and makes a mock-surprised face. Then she smiles. Johnny waves, but she's looking ahead again, tooling down the street until she disappears past the Masonic Hall.

Johnny doesn't see anything else for the next few minutes. He's remembering how they always gathered at her house, because it had a widow's walk with a view down the river, and how they'd sit up there and drink lemonade and joke with her parents—he envied her her parents—until they were ready to pile into her secondhand Pontiac and go off jitterbugging.

They were crazy about jitterbugging!

Alva Potter and Carolyn Mitchell and Earl Blake Jr. and Dinah Swain and Mike Mitchell and Lois Kilby and Susie and him. Roger Lambert, too, and whoever he was squiring around.

Graduation night there was one last expedition—they always called them expeditions—to the official town celebration at the Sahara, the best place ever for a bonfire. He remembers trying to dance on the sand and finally giving that up to sit talking together, and he remembers divulging that he and Earl Jr. and Alva Potter were planning to join the Navy. And how Roger Lambert trumped them by boasting that he'd already signed up, and not only that, but had been accepted for pilot training.

Johnny rolls his eyes to think that Lambert ended up with Susie.

But it was never going to be him. They'd been best friends forever, an accident of living across the street, and he remembers putting an arm around her that night and almost thinking they might kiss. But he hadn't dared try. She may have stayed a loyal friend, but he'd understood for a long time that Mr. and Mrs. O'Leary's little girl wasn't going to take up with someone who lived in *that* neglected house, with *those* awful parents.

He still wishes he'd tried, though. He never got another chance.

They went off to enlist a week later, Early driving him and Earl Jr.—Alva Potter had backed out at the last minute—to Portland. And now he remembers coming back from the recruitment office to find Dinah sobbing on the porch, because she and Earl Jr. had gotten married the day before, and now she didn't want him to leave. And he remembers Earl Jr. taking her in his arms and telling her everything would be all right.

When Early drives into the yard Eric drops the ax and wipes his hands on his jeans. Then he walks over, tipping his head to see if there's anyone else inside the Valiant. But Early gets out of the car by himself.

Then James comes out onto the porch.

"Did you take Primus inside?" Early says.

"Yeah, he needed to lie down."

Early looks at Eric.

"I couldn't get him to come along without spilling the beans. You ready for plan B?"

"Sure," Eric says. "I guess so."

"Hop in, then. No time like the present."

Eric opens the door and gets into the front.

"Mind if I go?" James says.

"More the merrier."

Early opens the driver's door, and James squeezes past him into the back. Early gets in and backs them around and they head out the driveway to the River Road.

"How long's it been?" James asks Eric.

"Oh, God. Since I was fifteen?"

"What are you going to say?"

"I'll think of something," Eric says.

It's gotten cool in the breeze, and Johnny is reaching to close the window when he spots the old Valiant at the top of Knox Street. He leaves the window up and sits forward, wondering if Early's decided to give him one more chance.

He hopes so, and thinks maybe he'll go, if that's the case.

But when the Valiant shoots across and parks in front of the hardware store, there are three of them who climb out. There's Early, and that must be young James, who looks a lot like Earl Jr., and there's a third fellow, a rangy guy who slaps his hands on his hips and grins lopsidedly at the other two men.

They all turn at the same time and look up at Johnny's window.

But they don't see Johnny, because he's already on his way into the kitchen. He's stepping over the sea bag and standing near the door, a little short of breath, a bit dizzy from the sudden movement.

He listens as they start up the steps. Then they're on the landing, making it creak.

Johnny waits, holding his breath, but nothing happens. It goes quiet and nobody moves. He leans closer, and when three firm knocks finally come, it makes him jump. But he recovers quickly and pulls the door open. And sees his son grinning back at him, flanked by Early and James.

"Mordak," Eric says then, "we come in peace."

Which puzzles Early and young James, you can see it in their faces.

But which strikes Johnny as just perfect.

"Age before beauty," Eric says, and gestures for Johnny to climb into the shotgun seat.

Then he and James squeeze into the back. Early punches buttons and backs away from the curb. He makes a blatantly illegal U-turn on Main Street and points the Valiant down Knox. They ride past the church and turn onto the Speedway and go past the house sitting up on its high bank. When they cross the bridge Johnny looks back at Eric.

Eric nods. "I remember."

"What's that?" James says. He was looking out the other way.

"Nothing."

"Don't tell me nothing."

They go back and forth, pretending to argue, and Johnny turns around, feeling warm, like something has thawed inside him. They bump off the bridge and Early steers the Valiant doggedly up a hill. The road levels off on the other side and drifts up close to the river and Johnny watches it flicker behind the trees, silvery in the fading light.

"How's old Primus doing, anyway?" he thinks to ask.

"Not bad, for a hundred years old."

"He's a hundred?" Johnny says.

"Just last month."

"Imagine sticking around for a hundred years."

"Well," Early says, "you'll be dead a lot longer."

"There's that," Johnny says.

They ride along for another mile and a field opens up. Primus's old barn appears with its faded red roof. Behind it is still the river, and there's just enough light left to see how it widens and deepens on its way to the bay.

An Interview with Jim Nichols

1. ***Closer All the Time*** **stitches together stories from the lives of the inhabitants of Baxter, Maine, all of whom seem to be pretty ordinary—at least on the surface. What aspects of character bring them together and force them apart?**

It all comes down to that fumbling around to find someone. It seems we're all born with this longing; we're made to think that someone exists for each of us, but we're not given the best tools to find them. So we knock around, dodging various obstacles like bad families and wars and accidents and illnesses, searching and hoping. We're handicapped in that we don't have a way to truly see into another's heart, and we can't ever communicate without approximation; it's this sort of haplessness that makes for the comedy and tragedy of our lives. A few of us are lucky, some make do while keeping an eye out, others are heroic and never give up, and there are those who despair and quit altogether. I hope in *Closer All the Time* there are examples of all of these categories, along with some of the comedy and tragedy.

2. You have a knack for portraying people who are down and out. What experiences have you had that have informed your writing?

Well, I grew up in a small, blue-collar town, and the advantage to this is that you know everyone, so the down-and-outers are not strangers. You know them and their families and their history. I'm sure that helped. And then, also, I've worked various hardscrabble jobs: I've been a cabbie, a bartender, a club singer; I've built fences, worked in a shoe shop, and on a dairy farm. I've drunk too much, gotten in fights, been in jail. I traveled for a time in circles that contain a fair sampling of the down-and-out. There but for the grace of God, etc.

3. In the book, many of the relationships are entangled. How does this relate to your understanding of small-town living, and, in particular, small-town New England life?

Closer All the Time takes place between World War II and the computer age, when things were a lot more static. People grew up, went to school, and then to work in the same little town (or in a neighboring town). In many instances you married someone you'd known since childhood, and if the marriage didn't work out, you married someone else you'd known since childhood and your ex-spouse married someone that all three of you had known! It's just the small-town-ness. I know tracing back my own family, you'd find a Nichols marrying a Pomeroy, and then their grandchild Nichols marrying another Pomeroy. And so on. In such a closed system there are bound to be complicated relationships, don't you think?

4. The characters in this book are very different in age, gender, and life phase, and yet in a way they are united in their own sense of alienation. How were you able to embody such varied

and different characters? Was it difficult to write from so many points of view?

It's just a function of observing, of listening. I think if you've paid enough attention and you're persistent, the characters will reveal themselves, and you'll recognize them from real people you've observed. Some act or comment will open them up for you, and from there it's just a matter of getting to the longing place and writing from there.

5. Do you sympathize with Johnny Lunden? How does he change over the course of the book?

Oh, I do sympathize with Johnny. He has a good heart, and he doesn't let it go sour despite the challenges he's faced since childhood. For example, he can be halfway into a life-defining tailspin and still recognize and share a secret wink with another lost child. Johnny gets a chance to change for the better at the end of the book, thanks to circumstance, his own courage, and the help of an unlikely angel, and we can only hope he succeeds.

6. Why is the idea of Baxter, Maine, so central to these stories? Is setting an important device for you as a writer?

Baxter as it exists in the book fixes the various stories to a particular time and place: small-town Maine in the years after World War II. Having it be a river town gave me a way to physically connect lives and stories, to help make everything part of a whole. The river is there at the beginning and at the end, and it frames Johnny

Lunden's book-long presence in what I hope was a resolving sort of way.

7. The role of family is an important subtext in this book, either through blood or proximity. What does the concept of *family* mean to you? How do you relate it to the larger themes in the book?

This goes back to question number one for me, with the concept contracted a bit to focus on members of a family, rather than the whole of humanity. But it's the same thing, really—our tragic (and funny) inability to communicate accurately, and the resulting difficulty in connecting.

8. The characters in *Closer All the Time* all seem to be longing for something. How does this reflect your larger ideas about American culture and society?

I think that like everybody, the characters in the novel just want a place in the world and someone to share it with. Even in good families, that safe place a child inhabits only lasts for so long, and then adolescence arrives and the longing begins.

9. You are an award-winning short-story writer. How was writing *Closer All the Time* different for you?

Most of the chapters in *Closer All the Time* were written as stand-alone short stories, but when it came to publishing them as a book, my editor suggested I try and interconnect them to make the book more of a whole. I found this to be a very interesting process, discovering similar characters and circumstances that I could conflate, inventing ways to carry them through a novel-size breadth of experience. It was a process full of surprises and delights that I really enjoyed. I did have to write three new stories, or chapters, and I had to insert other references and transitions. My previous book was a novel, so I had that experience to fall back on when it came to the expanded scope and different skills involved.

10. How has living in rural Maine impacted your writing, if it has?

I like to write about the people I meet or hear about, from their point of view (rather than that of an outside observer), which definitely has an impact on vocabulary and vernacular. These are the folks I'm interested in, and their voices sing to me. I want to tell their stories the same way they'd tell them.

11. There is a pervasive sense of claustrophobia in this book; how do your characters free themselves from it?

Some, by going out on the river in the fog; others, by giving up control of their lives; others, by sneaking around where nobody is looking. One flies small airplanes through the snow and gloom. Another pretends she's a famous actress instead of a housewife in a stunted marriage. One boy pushes eagerly into that adolescent emotional separation from his family, another just runs away from home, while a third opens his heart to the wider world his grandfather knew.

12. What elements of your characters' personalities are revealed in their relationships? Who is your favorite character, and why?

I think when you tell anyone's story you reveal neediness; heart, or lack of same; courage or weakness; resolve; kindness—whatever dominates. There are bound to be opportunities in all directions, and characters will respond in one way or another. As for my favorite character, I've spent so much time with them that I love them all, but my favorite would have to be Early Blake. Early was a late arrival on the scene (his was the first additional chapter I wrote), but he made his continued presence inevitable, and second only to Johnny's in importance. I love how he turned out. Early was someone who always seemed to get where he absolutely needed to be with a minimum of fuss.